MW01377861

The Family Experiment

Mayank Chamoli

Ukiyoto Publishing

All global publishing rights are held by

Ukiyoto Publishing

Published in 2022

ISBN 9789357878647

This is a work of fiction. Names, characters, businesses, places, events, locales, and incidents are either the products of the author's imagination or used in a fictitious manner. Any resemblance to actual persons, living or dead, or actual events is purely coincidental.

www.ukiyoto.com

Contents

The Seed of doubt is sown

What comes to mind when you hear the word "Experiment"?Well, most of us would start thinking about the experiments we did during school or college days or maybe recall some experiments done by famous people to achieve some amazing results. I don't want you to recall any experiment you have in your memory but focus on this Family Experiment which you are going to read about. Well, this experiment is conducted by Amar, with emotions full of pain, love, care, fear, and many more.

Well, those who are wondering What does his name mean? Let me clarify for you, it means immortal. His memory resembles his name, as it is long-lasting, and because of that, he sometimes finds it difficult to get over certain things. He was a late bloomer from a young age, as he learned many things later than most people of his age. For example, he learned to ride a bicycle at the age of 13, whereas most of his friends learned it at the age of 10. Some of you might think that he has had a learning disability since he was young, but its not. Things around him were not able to produce the desired situation where he could learn many things when others were learning . For example, Getting a bicycle at the age of 13 would have never helped him to learn it at the age of 10.Resources were late to arrive, not his ability to grasp or learn them.

Not only is he a late bloomer in many things in life, but he is also late in realising that fact as well. How comic! He realised this after amassing a large number of academic papers but still being unable to find work. It has been three years since his last day of college, and his college memories are getting faded as well. He is going through a pressure tunnel created by his own expectations and finding no sign of light at the other end of it, but he is going in the hope of surpassing it. Pressure, frustration, and fear of failure are trying their best to put him under tremendous pressure, but like most Bollywood movies with happy endings, he is hoping for a similar result in his life.

Now a few of you might be struggling to portray him in your mind. Well, let me help you with that. He is an average-height, lanky gentleman with better intelligence than most of his friends. Remember, I said intelligence, not academic results. There is a difference between those two things. His intelligence is the sole reason his family has high expectations from him though they never expressed it openly to him . He suffers from imposter syndrome at times because he can't accept the fact that, despite being labelled intelligent since childhood, he is struggling to make a few dollars. Oh yeah! Dollars are used rather than INR because of his truly global aim. That's all about him, as we try to look at the other people with whom he lives. In summary, it is a four-member Indian middle-class family. They have some big hopes for the future, the pressure of those hopes, some specters, but a very positive attitude.

The head of the family is his father, whose name is Nischint, which means free from worries or sure about things. He is within touching distance of 60, and his facial expressions suggest that he is indeed Nischint (worry-free). He works at a sugar mill as a manager, but he never gave that impression. Don't take it in a negative way! He always worked as if he is the owner and being very attentive and punctual at work. Work is worship, which is what he radiates from his passion and devotion towards it.

Second in command is Mrs. Mamta, which means "love of a mother or motherhood." A strong house manager with excellent money management skills. Every penny saved by the family demonstrates her financial prudence. She could be referred as the family's Chief Financial Officer (CFO).

Now we move to the youngest member of the family, and that is Amar's sister, named Sanskriti, which means "tradition" or "custom." She is still in school and soon will be transitioning into college life. She is not only intelligent but also possesses skills like painting and cooking, though she has no intention to make a career as a chef.

Now we have a good idea about each member of the family, but there is one more character who will appear to disrupt things very soon, otherwise things were going quite smoothly in the family. Hold on! Before we take a plunge into his characteristics, we have to understand the sequence of events that led to that disruption. To understand it, let's go back to the beginning. Yes, back to Amar and his life.

Before enrolling in an engineering program, he tried a variety of activities with which he struggled to connect. Because his neighbours come from various walks of life, he must listen to a few of them. He attempted and failed the army officer examination twice. The same fate was there with the entrance examinations for top engineering colleges. Those few months felt like he was in love with something, broke up with it, then pursued someone new and met the same fate. He moved on from that love story when he enrolled at a nearby engineering college. Despite the fact that it was expensive, the family was able to pay the fees. I am not rewarding anyone who could guess how was it possible. We all know it was due to Chief Financial Officer's wise savings and spending money on things that were needed rather than 30% off but unnecessary items.Well, the Chief Financial Officer deserved the much needed designation ,and by now we all know why.

Throughout his four years of engineering, he was put under pressure not only by the difficulty of the course, but also by the constant selection of engineers for insanely expensive packages at big tech companies. Since receiving the fragrance of those large MNCs' (multinational corporations) packages, he can't wait to taste the entire pie of it.That was the first time Amar felt that his expectations weighed more than his own weight. Expectations were raised even higher because he is described as intelligent.These expectations played a dual role in his life. They not only put him under pressure but gave him a sense of confidence that, though it might be tough to get a job in an MNC (multinational corporation) but if he got that, then surely it was going to be a big lottery or a jackpot. When he was in his last year of engineering, he tried to get through multiple MNC interviews but couldn't get through any of them, though he was offered jobs in a few companies, but he didn't take any of them as he was after MNCs and their big packages.The intoxication of big packages from MNCs was so high on his mind that he never looked at those job offers that were given to him by non-MNCs. Few of his friends took non-MNC jobs because they believed that gaining experience was critical at that age and after 3–4 years, they would eventually land in an MNC.I am sure that you are well hooked and remember his characteristics.

The first year after degree completion was wasted sending resumes to various MNCs, hoping to land a job at one of them.Second year, finally the big package intoxication went down, and he struggled to find work because no company would hire someone with no experience and a full year of Gap. During second year, It seems like those non-MNCs that he rejected a year earlier were taking revenge by rejecting him.

The third year after graduation was the most difficult for him, and he tried many things other than applying for jobs, such as blog writing and even social media, but nothing worked out. The fear of failure started creeping up in his mind and he started having depression and anxiety. He started spending most of his time in the room in front of his computer applying jobs and looking for other things he could start to make some money. He stopped talking to all of his college friends and lost most of his outside connections. In this while he developed the fear of getting asked what are you doing in life by neighbours so he started staying in as much as possible. In a few months time, he felt completely isolated and was living in prison with no intention of walking out. This lack of connection with the outside world could have gone on forever, but then comes our catalyst, who will change the whole scenario. For those of you who are wondering what a catalyst is, it is something that helps two or more chemicals react without participating in the reaction. How did it happen? Hold on, we are slowly progressing towards it.

It was one fine evening, fine because the weather was really nice, but Amar has nothing nice going on in his life. There was a knock on his house's entrance door. After a while, Amar's mom shouted, "Amar, your friend is here." When he heard it, he was shocked, as it has been a long time since any of his friends have visited him. He quickly got ready and went out to see who it was.

Oh, Samridh, how are you? Amar asked his friend a question.

(Samridh means Prosperous or wealthy)

I am doing okay, and how about you, Amar? Samridh responded with a question as well.

"Nothing spectacular. It is like counting days rather than making days count."

Samridh was astonished to hear this from Amar's mouth, as Amar was someone he always looked at as a very smart and mentally tough guy.

What happened to you? It has been almost 7 years since we last met, said Samridh.

Those 7 years flew by at such a breakneck pace that I didn't get time to react. It has been a swing between my engineering degree and my quest for a job. It seems like 7 years have taken more than half of my lifetime, Amar replied, with disdain clearly written on his face.

Samridh wasn't expecting that kind of reply and tried to further dig into the matter as he wanted to understand exactly what went wrong with Amar.Before he could ask anything further, Amar asked him to come in as they were still at the door.After they had settled down, Amar told him the entire story, from the time he started college until now, and how much pressure he is under. After hearing his story, Samridh was lost for a while, which is when Amar asked him what happened.

I think my decision to not invest in education was right after schooling,replied Samridh.He further said, "See, Amar, I didn't spend a single penny on my tertiary education and used that money to feed my business idea."

What business idea? asked Amar with curiosity.

I started off supplying groceries to a very small hotel, and with constant efforts, now I am supplying groceries to 10 big hotels and about two dozen restaurants.

Wow, you have built a successful business from the ground up in 7 years and still going strong, said Amar with a smile and pride.

Thank you, and you could have been my business partner had you listened to me 7 years ago when I suggested this business idea to you, Samridh responded with a kind of disappointment.

Well, yeah, I understand what you are trying to say, but back then, I was captivated by MNCs and their big packages and never thought about starting my own business, said Amar.

I believe it is still not too late, as I am planning to start a new business of supplying flowers to various hotels and restaurants. You could join me with some capital, and we could use your intelligence to grow it quickly as well. I know you passed up the business opportunity 7 years ago, but I am offering it to you again, Samridh said, presenting a business proposal.

It sounds great, but as you know, I have spent a significant amount of money on my studies and am not earning right now, so I can't say yes immediately. I need some time to think about it, and I also need my family's approval, as they will be funding my this venture as well, replied Amar.

I understand your situation, and I am not in a hurry as well.I would also need some time to arrange enough funding to start it off, explained Samridh.

I think I need to leave now to prepare some receipts for tomorrow's grocery order and collect some orders as well. Take care, Amar, and please consider my business proposal as well.

Thank you, Samridh, and I will let you know soon , replied Amar.

Nothing but Confusions

Once Samridh left, Amar went to his room and started thinking about what should be his next step. Should I join Samridh and start a new life, or should I still keep trying to look for a job?At this point, Amar could feel that his personality has been split into two distinct personalities, where one suggests that he takes a new start in life where he could work hard with his friend and start making money, which would help him to get stress-free, and the other suggests that he keeps his focus on finding a job as targeting multiple things could be proven fatal, and investing money in business could bring him more stress and frustration.

The whole night, those things kept on going in his mind, and he found difficult to sleep. The next day, he even took a pen and paper to write pros and cons to understand it better, but sadly, he can't convince himself to invest in business right now.Days and weeks passed, and that business idea slipped out of his mind, and he never contacted his friend to say yes or no about it either.One day, Amar's phone rang. It was his friend, Samridh. He thought that Samridh must be calling to know about his decision regarding new business.

When he answered the phone, Samridh asked him if he was available tomorrow to accompany him on a trip to a hotel where he was going to negotiate a business deal for supplying flowers. Amar was trying to avoid any kind of question regarding that investment plan, so he quickly said yes and hung up the phone. The next day, he met with Samridh early in the morning and went to the hotel he talked about yesterday. This is the first time in many years that he has stepped out to go that far. The hotel manager welcomed both of them and had a nice interaction. The way the manager spoke to them and treated them showed Amar that his friend has a good reputation in the business world. When Samridh closed the deal, the manager offered them a free lunch as well.

On the way home, Samridh said something to which Amar couldn't relate. He said that,See Amar,this world respect the money or the status you have in the society.You saw how that manager treated us nicely with respect and even offered food just because I am a well-established supplier in the market. Had we gone there as an amateur supplier, we would have been waiting for at least a couple of hours, and I can guarantee you that not even a glass of water would be free there. I am not sure what kind of respect or status you have in your family, Amar, but my family started giving me respect or taking my opinion seriously as I started making money. I still remember the first year of my business journey. It wasn't easy at all, and I incurred some minor losses as well. My family started doubting my abilities and gave me a hard time. Finally, in the second year, I made first profit, and they were overjoyed. Samridh kept on speaking, whereas Amar was struggling to get anything out of it as he had never experienced anything like this in his family.

Amar didn't realise that it has been more than 30 minutes since they left the hotel and reached his house.All Amar could say while getting out of Samridh's car was "bye," as he was experiencing some deep thinking.It was almost evening, and he was having a severe headache due to deep thinking. He told his mom that he was going to take a nap and went to his room. Somehow he was able to put his mind at rest and took a couple of hours of nap.Once he got up, it was almost night time. He skipped dinner in order to write things that drew parallels between his life and Samridh's life.

After writing a few pages and spending significant time, he came to the conclusion that there is a big difference between how his family thinks Vs. how the Samridh family thinks.He was standing in front of a mirror and was talking to himself as if he was trying to explain things to a different person.

" I think his family is more pragmatic and lacks empathy. They might not be emotionally attached to him and expect a result rather than seeing his efforts. They may exhibit this behaviour because he has had all of the resources since childhood, including a bicycle, a television, and even electricity."

“I think you are absolutely right. There is no comparison between you and him, or even between the families. You were 8 years old when you got electricity in the house for the first time, and you have only one childhood picture, which was taken when you were 3 years old. Look at him. He must have had electricity and TV since he was born and even gotten a car at an early age. He learned how to drive at the age of 15, and you are 25 and still don't know the ABCs of driving, and you remember he showed you his childhood pictures when you were in school with him.”

"Absolutely correct. That's why his family has less patience with him and my family has more because my family understands that I was given the resources quite late, so they can wait patiently to see me succeed.”

"Yes, and one more thing....

Amar, what are you doing? I can hear noises coming from your room, Nischint said.

Nothing, Papa. I am watching YouTube and listening to songs, Amar replied.

He suddenly realised that he was completely lost while talking to himself, and he must have been loud enough to be heard by his father.

"I think I should go to sleep now as it is late.What am I doing? I think I need to stop talking to myself or I will go crazy.”

He went to bed quickly as he was exhausted from being out for so long, which was unusual for him.He had a good sleep and woke up the next morning later than his usual waking time.

Once he walked out of his room, his mother asked, Are you okay, Amar?

Yes, I am okay, replied Amar.

She further asked him, "Have you paid electricity and water bills?"

I haven't paid them yet because I was gone out yesterday. Don't worry, I'll settle them tomorrow and will deposit the money into my bank account as well, Amar responded.

I believe your health is not in good shape,please allow me to ask your papa to take you to the doctor, suggested Mamta.

I believe he is running late for work, replied Amar.

"Amar, life will always be in a hurry, but we have to prioritise things." Sanskriti is preparing my lunch, and it will be enough to get you to the doctor and back, said Nischint.

Amar went to the doctor with his father, and to his surprise, by the time they came back home, his sister was still not done packing lunch.

What did the doctor say? Mamta asked Amar, as she couldn't ask this to Nischint due to him getting late for work.

Nothing serious. Just a slight drop in blood pressure due to stress and anxiety, replied Amar.

Why are you getting stressed, beta (son)? Things will be alright. Go have your breakfast, eat your medicine, and take some rest, suggested Mamta to Amar.

Amar took his breakfast and went to his room to rest. Sanskriti came to his room to give him medicine because he had forgotten to take it. He realised how caring his family is while eating medicine, despite the fact that he doesn't make a dime. The entire family became involved as soon as they learned that he was not feeling well, despite the fact that he was fine and that the slight drop in blood pressure was due to anxiety and stress.

"I think Samridh got the wrong idea about his family that earning money helped him gain status and respect in it. If that were true, I wouldn't be enjoying the centre stage in my family, where everyone is concerned about me, or maybe my family is just different."

Now Amar has decided not to think about it, as he has contemplated a lot about it and feels that his family is way different than his friend's family, and that is reflected in the way his friend Samridh explains as well.

He spent the rest of the day resting and enjoyed a good dinner with family, with each member asking about his health as well. The next few days went by, and he didn't realise that he was supposed to settle electricity and water bills and also needed to visit the bank to deposit cash. After 5 days, when that thing finally popped up in his mind, he quickly paid those bills online and asked his mother to hand him over the cash that needed to be deposited in the bank. He went to the bank to deposit money, and while on the way back home, he saw the message on his phone that reads: "Your account balance is 500,050 INR." He was amazed at how his family, with a little bit of saving every month, has saved 500,000 INR. As he reached home, he said to his mother, You won't believe mama, but we have saved over 500,000 INR.

All thanks to your father, who earned enough that we are able to save 500,000 INR, replied Mamta.

At this point, he began to consider that if he was also earning money, these 500k could have grown to 1 million as his earnings boost the saving.

As he was going through it, suddenly his mom interrupted, Where are you, lost beta(son)?

Nothing mom, is all Amar replied.

We are going to decide what to do with this saving at the dinner's table today, Mamta informed Amar.

Wow, that excites me, Amar responded.

Well, you could give your opinion about how that money can be used, Amar, said Mamta.

Okay Mom I will do my best with it.

After that, Amar went to his room and was lost in his own world as he said to himself, "Look at my family. I have made no contribution to family's income for so many years, yet my opinions are welcomed by them to know how to utilise the saving."

"Amar, you are a very lucky guy."

He spent the rest of his day thinking about how that saving could be utilised. Finally he has found the answer to that question.

"Education is very important in life, even if it is difficult to earn money after collecting enough educational papers. Since I had tertiary education, Sanskriti deserves to have tertiary education as well, but I don't want her to join the engineering or medical fields. She should join an art college to sharpen her painting and drawing skills and make a successful career out of that. According to my parents, it would be an unusual field to work in, but I should support her in her future endeavor.That's the right approach."

Finally, everyone has gathered around the dinner table in the evening.Mamta began a conversation while they were eating, "Do you know that our saving has reached 500k Nischint?"

Well, that's amazing, thanks to you, Mamta, replied Nischint.

I think we should spend at least half of the amount on buying jewellery for Sanskriti, which she can use in her marriage as well, suggested Mamta.

I think there is still significant time left in her marriage, and we should use this money to renovate this house first as it gets some water leakage in the rainy season, Nischint presented his idea.

I would like to buy some dresses and possibly a new phone, Sanskriti stated with a smile.

Amar beta(son), What do you think? Whose suggestion do you agree with? asked Nischint with a laugh.

I think he has some other ideas about how to use this money, said Mamta.

Whatever idea you have, we are ready to listen, requested Nischint to Amar.

I think we should be spending this money on tertiary education of Sanskriti. I have seen her paintings, and she has immense talent in them. I suggest she joins an arts college once she is done with school. Since there are only 15 months left for her schooling to be done, we keep them safe for her. As we all know, education is becoming increasingly expensive, so that amount should cover her art college tuition, Amar explained.

What do you have to say about Amar's suggestion, Miss Sanskriti? asked Nischint in a casual style.

"First, I would like to say wholehearted thanks to Bhaiya(brother), for putting my dreams and ambitions first and trusting my potential." I always wanted to explore this field but never had that kind of confidence to share it with you all and seek permission to join an art college after finishing off my school, replied Sanskriti.

I think it has been decided how this money is going to be used, and Sanskriti is going to Art's college after schooling, Mamta said to Nischint, to which he nodded.

Can we finish dinner now as we've been talking for so long? Nischint asked everyone.

Sure, sure, why not? said Amar in response.

They finished dinner quickly after that, as it was late in the night.As they all proceeded to sleep, Amar literally praised himself, saying that he was right about his family and that money is not the number one thing they want in life. Love, affection, care, and mutual respect are what glued them together.

"You are absolutely right, Amar. Didn't you see how quickly they agreed on your suggestion of utilising that money for Sanskriti's tertiary education?"

"Of course, my suggestion was aligned with her future achievement as well. She needed to be independent in the future, and surely doing what she likes can pave the way for her."

"Yeah, that is the point. Samridh might be doing very well with money, but surely his family lacks the correct emotional approach. As he shares his business journey with you, I believe you should share your family's unique bonding with him to give him a different perspective than the one he has, which revolves around money only."

"Yeah, that is what I should do but How am I going to bring this topic up to him since I can't call him and start giving a sermon that draws a comparison between money and human values?"

"I think you should call him one day, see if he is free, and go to a place to hang out. During that time, you might start a discussion on this topic."

"I think that's a good idea."

After having a self-discussion, Amar decided to give his mind some rest and went to sleep. Since his mind was clear due to his long self-discussion, he slept quickly and had a good sleep. The next few days went by, and he didn't think at all about the things he was thinking about a couple of days ago. Then one day he decided to call his friend Samridh to see if he was free to visit the nearby mountains to see snowfall.

Samridh informed him that he would be busy this weekend and would do his best to visit nearby mountains with him the following weekend. Amar realised that there was more than a week left before he was going to meet his friend, so it would be better not to stress his mind about anything related to what he was going to discuss with his friend. He started applying jobs again and got busy with his own things. Weeks went by, and Samridh never called to confirm anything. Amar also forgot about it and never tried to ask him.

One day, Amar's phone rang, and he saw that it was his friend Samridh.

He picked up the phone and said, Hey, Samridh, how are you?

I am alright, and I hope you are good as well.I am sorry that I got busy with my work and totally forgot about it.

About what? asked Amar with a surprise.

I think that thing has slipped out of your mind also.Remember how you suggested we go to the nearby mountains almost a month ago? Remember that ? said Samridh.

I remember it now, Amar replied.

I would be free this upcoming weekend. Let's go and enjoy some time on the mountains. Okay? Asked Samridh.

Yes, that's fine. See you soon, said Amar before hanging up the phone.

He realised after he hung up the phone that he doesn't feel great about going to the mountains because there is no more snowfall there, but then he remembered why he decided to meet him a month ago.

"I think you should go at least once to get his opinion on it, and prepare to be stressed because you will be thinking about it a lot."

"Absolutely true, but I have no other way to do it."

"Okay, let's see what happens and what he would say about it."

Finally, the day has arrived when Amar and Samridh are going to meet. He showered early in the morning and got ready as well. As soon as Samridh came, Amar quickly got into the car, and they were off to the nearby mountains.

On their way to the mountains, Samridh asked Amar,So what is your future plan? Are you going to keep looking for a job or move toward business?

I think I will stick to keep searching for a job, replied Amar.

What happened with the business idea?Did your family say no to investing in the business? asked Samridh with curiosity.

I didn't ask them because I think I can try for 6 more months to find a job and then look at other opportunities, Amar replied.

By the time they finished this interaction, they had almost reached the nearby mountains.They enjoyed the cool breeze and greenery before heading to the lake.Time flew by, and as soon as it hit 3 p.m.,the temperature began to fall.They decided to return home now because the mountains get dark very early in the evening.On the way back to their home, the topic again got some attention as they continued discussing it.

I believe it is better to start a business at a young age because it is hard to put things in place and takes a lot of physical effort. Once it starts going, it requires more mental work than physical work. That's why I am suggesting you start now and get it stable before you turn 30 years old,suggested Samridh.

Yeah, I understand that, but I feel I can still take 6 more months and try to find a job as things will not change drastically that could hinder my business if I choose to start it off 6 months later, replied Amar.

Don't you think your family members would ask you to do something else rather than just look for a job in these 6 months? asked Samridh with curiosity.

Amar saw this as the perfect opportunity to discuss in length the differences he has figured out between his family and the Samridh family.

I think there are some big differences between your family and mine, said Amar.

As soon as Samridh heard it, he pulled over his car as he felt there might be more concentration required on the discussion, and he doesn't want to get distracted while driving.

What do you mean by "big differences"? asked Samridh with a perplexed face.

See, you told me that you gained respect and status in your family after you started making money. That is one of the reasons you place more emphasis on making money, as you believe that earning money increases human value and respect in a family. My family never put any pressure on me to start making money or gave me any indication that doing so would boost my respect in the family. They have been very patient with me, though they ask sometimes about how my job search is going, explained Amar.

I think you haven't understood them.They could have been giving you hints in a roundabout way that you have been missing, said Samridh.

I don't like the suspense genre of movies, so kindly don't make it one now. Tell me clearly what you are trying to say, as I could not understand this indirect approach, clarified Amar.

Okay, let me try my best to explain it to you with some example, Amar, Samridh said.

Yes, please, Samridh, Amar replied.

Tell me what do you think is your monthly expenditure, asked Samridh abruptly.

After thinking for a while, Amar realised that he hasn't gone anywhere for proper holidays for so long. Since he is so busy with his own world, he doesn't buy new clothes or spend money on anything fancy.He is far far away from alcohol and smoking.

Suddenly Samridh interrupted him and said, what happened?

Well, As far as my understanding works,it hasn't changed much in these 7 years since we last met,Replied Amar.

Since you don't smoke or consume alcohol, don't go out anywhere, and are not a fashion fanatic, your monthly expenditure is very, very low, which your family can afford easily.Things are under control financially, plus you have a good image in their eyes, which is why they are not worried about you taking time, said Samridh with a smile.

You know me very well. I used to spend a good deal of my family's money on travelling and got into the habit of drinking alcohol during school days. Back then, I used to spend a significant amount of their money. So, as soon as I talked about starting a business, they expected me to start covering my own expenses, explained Samridh.

Still, I believe your expenses won't be that high, even with travelling and occasionally drinking alcohol, said a surprised Amar.

Yes, that is right. But do you remember what I told you about my first business experience?

Yes, I recall, Amar replied.

Well, before that first business failure, my family also had less pressure on me as they were paying only for my expenses. After school completion, when I told them that I wanted to invest the money, they kept it for my tertiary education, and then they were not happy with that. Samridh explained.

Why weren't they pleased with that? Amar inquired with curiosity.

I asked them the same question, to which they replied that it is tough to start a business at a young age and I might end up losing money and maybe never recover it, but with education you have better chances to recover money.I had to literally beg them to let me start off my business back then, said Samridh.

Yes, that is true, as in business, money makes money, and once you don't have money, you can't start any business, replied Amar.

This could be one of the reasons your family doesn't force you to get a job, as you have not incurred any business loss yet, and they have hope that one day, when you start making money, you will be able to recoup the money that is being spent on your education, suggested Samridh.

What about the respect and human values I experienced without even making money? Asked Amar.

These human values and respect go well with when you make money, or in your case, we could say that less monthly expenditure and not losing money in any business could be the strong reasons. Tell me one thing. If you need to buy something even worth a few pennies, do you seek your parents' consent? asked Samridh.

Yes, I always do, Amar replied.

Yes, that is what I am trying to tell you. You have no financial freedom and your monthly expenditures are well below the level.The day you try to gain this financial freedom through business and end up losing some of their money the human value and respect you are enjoying are going to take an infinite plunge.The day they find it difficult to meet the financial need of the house,surely they would ask you to start contributing financially in the family income. Whatever calmness you witness with them would be gone in a second, and whatever mistakes you have made all these while would be used by them to heavily diatribe you, said Samridh.

Once Amar listened to this, he started thinking about how his value and respect could fall so fast if he made any financial losses. He can't imagine his family criticising him that harshly. He was lost for a while but was suddenly interrupted by Samridh.

I have experienced it, so I can tell you that. Luckily for me, I used only half the money with my first business experience, so I had the other half to recover losses ,but during that period of recovering that money, they didn't even let me breathe properly. I was getting more criticism than food and water, said Samridh with a sheepish smile.

I still can't imagine that my family could go against me the way your family did, replied Amar.

Well, I understand your point of view because you haven't faced it, so it's hard to imagine for you, but trust me, the day you face it, you will remember my exact words, said Samridh as the closer line to end the conversation.

After that, they continued to drive towards Amar's house, and it didn't take much time to reach it.Once they reached,Amar got off and was so shaken by the interaction that he didn't even bother to say anything to his friend Samridh.He feels like a tree whose roots are cut off, and it can fall at any time. His beliefs about human values ,respect , and money have jumbled in his mind, and he is trying to segregate them. "The strong line he has in his mind to separate human values from money is gone."

Ignorance is bliss, but how long?

He got into his house, and as soon as he did, Mamta asked him how his trip to the mountains went. Before he could answer that, Sansriti asked, Do you need water? Bhaiya (brother), and he said no.

Yeah, it was great, and I enjoyed the nice natural beauty there, Amar replied to his mother.

Amar, get ready quickly. We are going to Yamraaj Uncle's retirement party, said Nischint with excitement.

(Yamraaj means the god of death though he is a very polite person and not scary at all)

I don't feel like going to the party now.I'm not as hungry as you are, so please go, Amar replied.

What happened to you again? asked Mamta.

I am okay. It is just that I am tired and do not feel like eating, replied Amar.

"If you are not coming with us, then we are not going as well," said Sanskriti.

"Yes, she is right," added Nischint.

After several requests from Amar, they finally prepared to leave without him after he ensures that he is fine and not hungry either.

While going, Mamta said, "If you don't feel okay while we are away, don't hesitate to call us."

Once they left, Amar realised that the turmoil in his mind related to human values versus money and respect calmed down as he could see that human values and mutual respect were shared by his family.As he was feeling calm now, he decided not to think about it more . He started looking for jobs online to distract his mind and got so caught up in applying for jobs that didn't realise a couple of hours had passed.

Suddenly, he heard someone entered the house and went out of his room to see who was there. He was surprised to see his family, as he didn't expected them to return so quickly.

He asked his sister, What happened, Sanskriti? Why have you all returned so quickly?

Yes, Mama (Mother) wasn't feeling well because you were alone here. She wasn't having a good time at the party, so we came back soon. Even Yamraaj uncle was asking why you didn't come as he hadn't met you for so long, replied Sanskriti.

As soon as Amar heard it, he said, Mama, why were you so worried? I am grown up now and 25 years old. I can take care of myself even when you are not around. Sanskriti just told me that you were so worried about me at the party and didn't enjoy it at all.

"Children are always small for their parents; it doesn't matter how old they grow," replied Mamta.

When Amar heard it, he was speechless and so touched that his heart wanted to cry and hug his mother, but he restrained himself because he has just told her that he is an adult now.

"Surely Samridh is wrong with all his understanding of money, respect, human value, or even his family.He has failed to comprehend his family and may have exaggerated his struggles in order to become a hero."

"Yeah, I believe it so."

Amar, where are you lost and who are you talking to while looking at the wall? asked Nischint.

Nothing , I am okay, Papa (father), Amar replied with a smile.

Okay, Amar and Sanskriti, It is late enough to go to sleep now and have a good night, said Nischint.

Good night, Papa and Mama, replied Amar.

After this, Amar went to his room to sleep, and while lying in bed, he decided that, at least for the next few months, he needed to somehow avoid contact with his friend Samridh to avoid any kind of conflict in his mind because there is such a big difference between what Samridh said about money and respect in a family and what he is experiencing in his house.

“I am not totally denying what he said, as he cannot be lying and must be speaking from his experience, but I cannot deny what I am experiencing myself in my family."

"Yes, that is what I also believe in. It is important to listen to people who are speaking from their experience, but don't deny what you see and experience yourself. Since you have decided to look for a job for the next few months, then give your 100% concentration to that and get away from this respect, human values, and money battle."

"Yes, that's what I agree on."

Amar was having a self-discussion when he fell asleep unexpectedly and woke up straight away in the morning. He felt quite good due a good sleep as he was physically very tired. He had such a good sleep after a long time, and the last time he slept so tightly was in college.

"I think I need to start off exercising to get myself physically tired to have good sleep."

"Yes, why not? Start it off today.”

"Absolutely"

Amar, are you up? asked Nischint.

Yes, Papa, I am up, and good morning, replied Amar.

Good morning, Amar, said Nischint.

Then he went to his mother and said, I am thinking to start off exercising and need to eat healthy food.

Well, that is a good idea, as it would help you to de-stress, Mamta replied.

Do you need any equipment for that? she asked.

Well, I don't need any equipment right now because I'm just getting started, Amar explained.

Okay, and what about your diet? Mamta inquired further.

I do not think I need anything special, replied Amar.

I think you should eat oats and bananas.I have watched on TV that usually early gym starters have them, said Mamta.

As you say, Mom, replied Amar.

As he turned around, he heard, "Nischint, while coming back from work, do bring some oats and bananas," Mamta said to Nischint.

Okay, I will bring them, replied Nischint to Mamta.

"Papa is so amazing as he didn't even ask who would need that as I have not told him about my exercise plan," Amar thought in his mind.

Now he has started exercising and has become very active in his job-seeking mission. It's been a week, and he has noticed a few changes, such as better sleep and his mind not wandering about topics that make him anxious.

Time was passing at a rapid rate, and one month has passed. Amar was doing well with his exercise and job search as well.

"I think I am going very well with exercise, and if I get a job now, things will be settled very well for me, and...

His phone abruptly began to ring. As he held up the phone, he saw that his friend Samridh was calling.

He quickly picked up the phone and said, Hello, Samridh, how are you?

I am fine, and I hope you are doing good as well, said Samridh.

Yeah, I am okay, and how is your business running? asked Amar.

Yeah, it is going well, and I am planning to expand it. What about your job search and future plans? asked Samridh.

Well, I am still going with the quest, replied Amar.

Okay, as I have just said, I am expanding my business, and if you are interested in investing, then let me know, said Samridh.

As soon as Samridh said it, Amar realised that it has been quite a while since Samridh said it for the first time about investment, and Samridh is growing rapidly while he is stuck in the job quest.

Give me a few days and I will let you know, replied Amar.

After listening to this, the Samridh didn't say anything as he got his answer.

When Call was executed, Amar realised the next few days would be difficult because he had to decide whether to pursue the business proposal or continue looking for work. The topic he has been avoiding to discuss has come before him, and this time he couldn't escape from it as he told Samridh to tell him about his proposal in a few days.

"I think I need to control this brain storm and start exercising now."

"Yes, that's true, but when will you discuss it?"

"I will discuss it in the evening, but I don't want to discuss it in my room."

"Okay, Amar, I think you could go to Nature Beauty Park and discuss in peace as it is very quiet there."

"That's a good idea, and for now, let's do exercise."

After that, he finished his exercise and took an afternoon nap to get fully ready for a strong brainstorming session. He got up in the evening from his nap and took a shower to get ready to go to the park. As soon as he came out of his room and Mamta saw him dressed,

She asked, Amar, where are you going?

I am going to Nature Beauty Park for some walking and to enjoy some fresh air, replied Amar.

Well, that's a good idea, beta (son), but be home before it gets dark and make sure you are not staying there too long as it gets very cold in the evening, Mamta instructed.

"Okay, Mom," Amar said as he dashed out of the house.

He was in a hurry, so it only took him 15 minutes to get to the park.

Once he reached there, he realised that before self-discussion, he should walk for a while in the park to freshen his mind. He walked for almost 15 minutes before deciding to face the enigma and the reason he was here.

"How could you ask Mom and Dad for investment now as you are the one who suggested how to use that saved money?"

"But I can't be waiting and keep seeking jobs as well. I am getting a golden opportunity to invest in a well-established business, and since Samridh is my friend, he can easily teach me the fine lines of the business."

"How about Sanskriti? You are the one who suggested getting her into an arts college, and now you want to use that money for your needs. That's very selfish, Amar. You have already spent a large amount on your engineering degree, and you still want to invest the money saved for her higher education. Haven't you seen the joy on Sanskriti's face when she found out that she is going to an art college?”

"But I have also wasted a lot of time seeking jobs, and this is a good opportunity for me. There is more than a year left for her to join an art college, and I can invest that money now to make some profit by the time she joins an art college.I can request Samridh that I am going to invest money for the period of one year, and after that, I would withdraw the amount needed for her first year college fee, and I am sure Samridh would understand it too."

"What if anything goes wrong in the business and you lose money?"

"Yeah, that's my concern as well...

"More importantly, I don't think Mom and Dad would agree to your business investment. They would have if you hadn't suggested how to spend the money they have saved."

"So, what shall I do?"

" I think…

Before Amar could draw any conclusions, he realised it was getting dark and that if he stayed any longer here, his mother would start calling him. Amar decided it was time to go home and began walking in that direction.When he arrived home, he discovered that his father has returned from work.

As soon as he entered the house and started walking towards his room, Nischint asked him, How was your park walk as your mom told me about it?

Yes, it was good because I enjoyed the fresh air and bird chirping there, said Amar.

As he turned around, his mom suddenly said, You seem a bit worried, and I have been noticing this thing for the past few weeks. What is going on, Amar? Is there anything that is bothering you?

Nothing much, mama, it is my job search that makes me anxious sometimes, replied Amar.

I told you several times, Amar."Just do your best and let things go," Nischint advised.

"Okay, Papa, I'll keep that in mind," Amar replied before heading to his room.

Once he reached his room, he decided that was enough for today's discussion, and rather than getting worried, he should listen to his father's words and do his best to decide whether to go for business investment or keep looking for a job.

After that, he had his dinner, and off to bed to relax his mind and body. When he awoke the next morning, he had headache and didn't feel like exercising.

"I think I need to stop exercising for a few days until I get this puzzle out of my mind, as I won't be able to concentrate on exercise."

"I believe that's the right decision, Amar."

"I better go to the park in the evening to discuss this topic there again today."

"Yeah, that is a smart idea."

After this self-discussion, Amar applied for a few jobs, had lunch, and took a nap. He didn't feel well when he got up because of headache.

"I don't think I need to go to the park to have some thoughts about it, as it takes half an hour to get there and come back."

"Yeah, that is true. It's better if you relax in your room and discuss it at length."

Before he could further proceed with that, he informed his mom that he was not going for a walk in the park due to the cold weather out there so that she would not disturb him during his self-discussion.

"I think you should talk to mom about this and see what she says."

"Yeah, that's right, but you know she will surely discuss it with Papa, and then somehow Sanskriti will be getting that too. I don't want to disappoint Sanskriti at all."

"Then what is the solution? You can't be wasting anymore time as you need to answer Samridh in a day, and even if you say no to him, you still need to see that you have taken enough time to look for a job, and you can't take much time now."

"Yeah, and if things keep going like this then i think one day mama and papa would ask me when you're going to start contributing to the family income."

"Yeah, remember when Papa suggested using that saving to renovate the house because you can see paint peeling off the walls and some leakage during the rainy season as well. Mom also suggested jewellery for Sanskriti. After that money is spent on Sanskriti's education, they will need more money for house renovation and jewellery."

"Yes, so possibly there is no solution for it now, and I need to find a job to start contributing financially before mom and dad run out of patience."

"Yeah, that is the right approach, and you can tell Samridh that your family doesn't have any spare money to invest in business."

"Yeah, that's a good reason to give, and I hope he won't be too disappointed as well."

"He won't be, and kindly, call and inform him of your decision so that you won't keep him waiting."

"Yes, I will do it."

Amar has finally reached a conclusion after nearly an hour of self-discussion. After this, he didn't discuss anything further. Finally, the day has come when he is going to call his friend Samridh. He picked up his phone to call Samridh but was surprised to see that Samridh is calling him.

"He must be calling to ask me about my decision and expecting me to say yes about it, but sadly he has no idea that I am going to deny his polite business offer."

The call was dropped before he could come out of his self-discussion and pick it up.

Amar called his friend and said, Hey Samridh, how are you, my friend?

I am alright, my friend, and how about you? replied Samridh.

I am good, and I need to tell you something important , and I was about to call you as well, said Amar.

Yeah, that's alright, and I have something way too important to tell you, and it is a serious matter as well, replied Samridh.

What happened? asked Amar with a shock.

Things aren't going right in my business.Luckily, I didn't expand my business; otherwise, I could have faced a heavy loss, said Samridh.

How did it happen? Explain it to me thoroughly, Amar asked.

You know, due to the sudden change in weather pattern and extreme cold, the flower business has gone down as the growth of flowers in the local area has been bad and we need to get flowers from other cities.As supply has been affected, the profit has gone down, and I am planning to shut this business for the next 6 months, explained Samridh.

That's sad. I think due to climate change, weather patterns are not consistent, which are affecting flowers, crops, and fruit farming, replied Amar.

Yes, exactly, and I must say that you have been lucky with all this, said Samridh.

How am I so lucky? Amar asked, surprised.

See, I have been asking you to invest in the business, but you decided to take time. If you had invested when I first asked you, you would be in the same situation as I am today. Sometimes not doing something is better than doing something, explained Samridh.

Yeah, I can understand it, and I wanted to call you to tell you that I can't invest now as my family has decided to use the money we saved for Sanskriti's education, replied Amar.

"Thank goodness you didn't invest. Had you invested the money and lost it, your family would have made your life hell, and you would find extremely difficult to even survive in that house," said Samridh.

I don't think they would be that harsh on me even if I had invested and lost money, responded Amar.

I think you are still living in some kind of dreamland. This time you were lucky, but had you lost money in any business venture, you would see how they behave. I have faced it, so I can assure you about that, said Samridh.

Well, this is one thing I think we can't agree on, because I have never faced it, so I am not sure how they would react if something like this happened, Amar responded.

Yeah, I can understand your point as well. Since you have no interest in investing and the time is also not right to invest, you may take some more time to look for a job, suggested Samridh.

Yeah, that's all I can do for the time being, replied Amar.

Yep, okay, okay, I am going to finish off a few chores.I will call you next time if I get any update regarding business, okay? said Samridh.

Okay sure. See you soon, said Amar.

Amar breathed a sigh of relief when the phone call ended.

"Thank goodness I didn't invest and instead saved money. I still don't agree with him that, had I lost money, my family would be making my life hell. I think that is too much exaggeration."

"Absolutely, and since you don't need to be worried about that investment plan, you can focus on exercise and your job search."

"Yeah . What a relief I have now."

After this, Amar didn't pay much attention to what he had on his mind and got busy with his usual life.One day, when Amar was in his room, he heard his parents discussing something about him, but due to being in room, he wasn't able to hear what exactly they were saying except for a few words like "future" and "money".He wanted to be the part of the conversation or at least listen fully, so he walked out of his room.

As soon as he reached there, they changed the discussion topic which totally surprised Amar.

What are you discussing? asked Amar.

We are discussing what to do with the faucet we have in the kitchen as it is leaking, said his father, Nischint.

I think we better get it changed since it can't be fixed, suggested Amar.

This is what I have been suggesting to him for almost 15 minutes, replied Mamta.

After this, Amar turned around and went to his room.

"I am certain there was no discussion about the faucet.What does a faucet have to do with money and the future?"

"This is the first time they are hiding something from you. Why would they do it?"

"I think I need to find out, but how? Surely they won't be discussing it in front of me."

Amar was thinking of a way to get what they were talking about. Suddenly, he looked at the clock in his room. It was around 8 p.m. He recalls that when he got home from the park after walking, it was 6:30 p.m. and his father was home.

"I think I have got an idea. I will go to the park tomorrow and come back by 5:50 p.m. to hide myself outside the house near the window and listen to what they will discuss. Maybe it would take me a few days, but this is the only way I could hear what they were talking about, and hopefully they would discuss it again in the evening as Papa has very little time in the morning before he goes to work."

"This is the only way to get it, Amar."

The next day, he went out of his house, informing Mamta that he was going to park and would be back by 6:30 p.m. He did what he planned as he got back by 5:50 p.m. and hid himself outside the house near the window, from where he could hear what his parents are discussing. He realised that his father was not home yet. As he thought about going into the house, suddenly he heard the noise of someone entering the house.

"That must be papa," Amar said to himself.

Mamta, where are you? Amar heard his father calling for his mom.

Yeah, I am here.How was your work? asked Mamta.

It was fine, but I am feeling stiffness in my body due to the cold weather, replied Nischint.

I recommend taking a shower with hot water, and if you want, you could take a shower right now because the water heater is hot, Mamata suggested.

Okay, I am going for a shower.Kindly make me some tea and get today's newspaper as well, requested Nischint.

After this, Amar could hear his father walking towards the washroom.

“I think today they are not discussing it, but nevermind, I would try again tomorrow," Amar said to himself.

After this, he entered the house with the hope that , tomorrow he would be able to hear what his parents were hiding from him. He struggled to pass the time because he was so interested in learning more.

What and why are they hiding from me? Are they planning something else with the money we have saved? Should I go and ask them directly? Why didn't they ask my opinion about it? I think if I asked them directly again, they would hide it too, so there is no option but to hear them secretly.

These are the things going through Amar's mind before he finally fell asleep. When he awoke the next morning, he had only one thought: he would figure out what they were hiding. He doesn't feel like doing anything, including his usual things like exercising or applying for jobs.

"I'm hoping to solve this mystery today because this is the first time I have noticed that they are hiding something."

He remained in his room all day, anticipating the evening. He tried to sleep but, due to anxiety, he couldn't. Finally, the moment has come for which he has been waiting all day. He got out and went to the park, intending to return by 5:50 p.m. He got lost in his thoughts while in the park, and it was 05:45 p.m. by then that he realised and started walking towards the house.

"Damn! I am late now "

Due to his running, it took him only 10 minutes to reach his house.

As soon as he reached the house, he thanked God as he could see his father getting into the house. He took a sigh of relief and took his position behind the window to hear the whole conversation.

Where are Amar and Sanskriti now? inquired Nischint.

Sanskriti is in her room, and Amar is gone for his park walk, replied Mamta.

After listening to their conversation for a couple of minutes, Amar finally got to hear what he had been trying to find.

So, do you know what Amar is thinking about the future? Nischint asked Mamta.

I have no idea about his future plans, but he spends most of his time in his room and keeps applying for jobs on his computer, replied Mamta.

I mean, I will be retired in 3 years, and he needs to be earning well by then, said Nischint.

Yeah, and I think he must having these things in his mind for sure and worried about them as well, replied Mamta.

Should we talk about this with him as he needs to be aware of the current situation and he needs to start earning soon? Sanskriti is growing as well. Our whole saving would be used for her education. We need money for house renovation, buying jewellery for Sanskriti, and even to pay our medical bills as we both are getting older. He needs to understand that I won't be this young forever, Nischint said worriedly to Mamta.

Don't worry, Nischint. He is trying his best, and results will be out soon, said Mamta while assuring Nischint.

Yeah, but we do have our own patience limit as well. We can understand what he is doing, but sometimes it is very hard to explain it to other people. For example, most of my friend's children have started working, and whenever they ask me about Amar, I usually find myself speechless and always avoid this question, replied Nischint.

Your point is right, Nischint, but I am sure he is trying his best, and if we suddenly ask him about when he will start contributing financially, then he will come under severe pressure, said Mamta.

Yes, that is the enigma I am having in my mind, that if I ask him about when he will start making money, he gets under pressure, and if I don’t say it, then I find myself under pressure when people keep asking me what he is doing, replied Nischint.

I hope he would start making money soon so we would be tension-free about his future, he would be independent financially, and you won't be feeling speechless against questions related to him, replied Mamta.

Yes, I hope so as well, Nischint said.

As soon as Nischint stopped speaking, Mamta realised that it was almost 06:45 p.m. and Amar hasn’t reached the house yet.

Amar hasn’t come yet. Usually he is back by 6:30 p.m., but not today, Mamta said to Nischint.

Just call him, and you will get your answer about where he is, suggested Nischint.

As soon as Amar heard it, he panicked, and instead of putting his phone on silent, he ran away from the house. He would have hardly moved 25 steps away from the house , he could hear his phone ringing.

He picked it up, and before Mamta could ask him anything,"I'll be home in 2 minutes, mom," he said before hanging up the phone.

Right after a couple of minutes, he was in the house.

As he got into the house, Mamta asked him, How was your walk, and why did you get late to be back?

Yeah, it was good, and I got late as I was relaxing in the park after the walk and didn't realise what time it was, replied Amar.

After this, Amar continued his walk to reach his room.

"Tonight is going to be very tough for me as the pendulum of my understanding of things has swung in a completely opposite direction,"

Amar expressed no interest in having a family dinner and informed his mother that he was too tired to eat. He doesn't want to face the fact he heard today, though Samridh had given him an inkling many times.

"I was wrong all the while that they were not thinking about when I would start contributing money to the family income. I could see Samridh's frustration, but I was so caught up in my own understanding that I never tried to see it from a different perspective."

"It is about being ignorant of reality and trusting only what you are seeing, Amar. You should have decoded their concerns and issues behind their very patient and respectful behaviour towards you."

"I am not saying they are wrong, as their demands and expectations are right, but it has suddenly appeared that I can feel the real pressure of contributing financially for the first time in my life."

"Absolutely, it feels like that you are running out of options now and, at the same time, have to find the quickest way to start making money."

"You know very well that whenever I get under pressure, I always take the wrong decision .Even during my engineering subject selection, I succumbed to peer pressure and chose something in which I lacked confidence."

"How about Samridh's other saying that if you invested money and lost it, they would have made your life hell?"

"I don't want to even think about it.Had that happened the way he had described it, I would have either gone completely mad or died."

"I think Samridh was right that human values and respect get better with money. Right now, you can see Mama and Papa talking about you between themselves. Soon they will talk about it with you, and a few months later that question will become more frequent. When it happens, you will see that life is becoming hell, like Samridh had said."

"It appears that, and I should find work as soon as possible to stop that thing."

"I thi.......

Right at this moment, Amar realised that his face was sweating despite the room being cold enough.

As he tries to remove his sweater, he starts feeling cold . This is probably the first time that fear of failure has made him sweat even in cold weather. He looked at the clock on the wall. It is just ticking over 11 p.m.

"It has been a couple of hours since I started this enlightenment about money, human values, and respect. I better sleep now and try to find the answer to this conundrum by tomorrow."

As Amar slept later than his usual sleeping time, he woke up when he heard his mom knocking on the door.

What happened, Amar? Why haven't you been up?

Amar quickly responded, I am okay. It's just that I slept late last night, so I failed to get up on time."

He checked his phone and saw that it was 9 a.m., which was 2 hours later than his usual wake-up time. He quickly put on his sweater and got out of the room. Once he got out, he realised that only Mamta was in the house, whereas Papa had left for work and Sankriti was off to school as well.

Go take a shower, Amar, as you might still be sleepy, suggested Mamta.

Amar quickly went to the shower, brushed his teeth, and finished his late breakfast. He is all set to find the right balance between what was going on in his mind during the night.

"I think I am trying to solve too many issues at once. Rather than getting distracted again and again, I need to focus on one issue and try to solve it."

"Yes, as you are not getting into business, so forget about it. What you have heard from mama and papa is going to get more pronounced if you don't start earning. I believe you should focus solely on money earning, and observe how their behaviour changes."

"And if I start making money soon and their behaviour changes, it means Samridh was absolutely right."

"You need to fix your things. Even if he is proven right in the end, isn't that going to bother you a lot, or is it?"

"I better not think about whether it is going to bother me a lot or not; I will analyse it once I see it."

Testing the Conundrum

As he was going through his thoughts, he heard someone ringing the house bell. Before he could ignore it, Mamta said, Amar, go and see who is at the door as I am busy in the kitchen.

When Amar approached the door, he was surprised to see his uncle Yamraaj standing there.

Hello, Amar, How are you, my boy? My goodness, it has been so long since I last saw you, said Yamraaj with an astonished look.

Namaste (greetings), Uncle Yamraaj,I'm fine; how about you? Please come in, said Amar with a smile.

Mama, Yamraaj uncle is here. Please bring water for him, Amar said to Mamta.

So how is your career going on? asked Yamraaj.

He is trying his best to find a job but can't get it as of now, replied Mamta before Amar could answer it.

"Struggle is the key to success, and keep trying, Amar, as I am sure you will get it soon," said Yamraaj.

Thank you, uncle, for your appreciation, replied Amar.

I have a small request as well as an opportunity for you, Amar, said Yamraaj.

What is that uncle? Amar inquired, surprised.

A couple of weeks back, Akshat fell down while riding his bicycle and broke his left leg. He is now fine, but he will be unable to attend school or his tuition classes for at least one month. In two months, he is going to have his final exams. If he misses school and tuition classes for that long, he would find it very hard to pass the final examination. It would be great if you could teach your cousin Akshat for two months. I know you are more than capable of doing it, Amar, said Yamraaj with a worried face.

Surely Amar will help his brother to pass the exam, replied Mamta.

Amar, consider it your first job, as I would pay you whatever I was paying for his tuition classes, Yamraaj further added .

Amar, your uncle is giving you a great job offer, said Mamta with a laugh.

As you say, Uncle Yamraaj, said Amar with a smile on his face.

Okay, as you know, he can't walk, so every day you have to come to my house to teach him.I know it will be difficult, and I don't want you to waste your valuable time, so just bear with him for a couple of months as he will be done with his final examination in the next two months, Yamraaj replied.

Don't worry, uncle.I would help him in the best possible way, assured Amar.

Thank you, Amar Beta(son). So, when are you going to start teaching him?asked Yamraaj.

I will be there by 4 p.m., as it will take me about 30 minutes to get there as well.So,I may teach him from 4 to 6 p.m., replied Amar.

Thanks once again, Amar. You have relieved all of my anxiety. I will be ready to welcome you by 4 p.m. tomorrow, said Yamraaj with a big smile.

Yamraaj's uncle then left because he was in a hurry.

As soon as he left, Mamta said to Amar, Congratulations, Amar, on your first job as a teacher.

Thank you, mama, he responded with a laugh.

He totally forgot what he was thinking or going through before Yamraaj Uncle arrived. He was so happy that he didn't bother to think about it for the rest of the day. All of his concerns vanished in a matter of minutes. He had a good dinner with the whole family and got good appreciation from all of them for getting the first opportunity to make money. Finally, Amar is in bed now, and before he could sleep, he started thinking about what is going to happen in the next two months.

"Uncle has given me a good opportunity to start earning money and get that feeling of success. In the next two months, I will pay my full attention to the work I have in hands and stay worry-free."

"You also have the opportunity to test the Samridh theory that earning money increases family respect and importance."

"Oh yes, I didn't even think about it, but surely, it is a perfect opportunity to earn money, test that theory, and see how money earning motivates me."

"Amar, be ready to feel the thrill from tomorrow onwards."

"Yes, absolutely, but I should get some rest now because tomorrow will be a long day for me."

"Yes"

After that, Amar fell asleep and miraculously woke before the alarm could sound. He quickly got out of bed, freshened up, and had his breakfast. Mamta suggested him to prepare a few things for teaching by using Sanskriti's old books. He took almost the whole afternoon for preparation and realised it was 3:25 p.m. when Mamta asked him what time he is leaving. He quickly left the house and started walking towards his uncle's house. He was so excited that he didn't realise the time he took from his house to his uncle's.

Uncle Yamraaj and Aunt greeted him with a big welcome as he entered their house. It gives him the vibe of being a celebrity. After a quick exchange of "Hi" and "Hello," he is in his cousin's room. He quickly exchanged the basic questions related to greetings and well-being with his cousin. Amar planned out how to teach his cousin once he knew exactly what he needed. Amar became so engrossed in his teaching that it is over 6 p.m. Once he finished teaching,Yamraaj uncle asked him to stay longer and have some tea, but Amar refused as it was getting dark outside with a chilly wind. Once he got to his house, everyone was waiting for him.

As he entered the house, Mamta asked him, How was your first day of work?

Yeah, it was good, Amar replied.

That's a good start, Amar, said Nischint.

Thank you Papa, Amar responded.

After he rested for a while, he had a good dinner, and slept well without thinking about anything. This continued for five days and finally Sunday is here. He got up late on Sunday, and interestingly, no one knocked on his door. He jumped out of bed, took a shower, and ate breakfast.

"After 5 days, I could sense the energy of someone who is working.Get up, do things, and have a peaceful sleep."

"Yes, and soon one month will be done, and your first salary will arrive. I think you should become a teacher, Amar."

"Yeah, I will see if I can teach Akshat well."

As he was going through his thoughts, Nischint asked Amar, Where are you? Please join us for lunch at the table.

Yes, I am coming there, papa, replied Amar.

Once he reached the table, everyone was waiting for him.

So how is your job going, Amar? asked Nischint.

Yeah, it is going well, papa, and I am enjoying it as well, replied Amar.

Yeah, it's good that you are enjoying your work, as enjoying it makes it easy, Mamta replied.

Bhaiya(brother), I would like to have a mobile phone cover with your first salary, said Sanskriti with a smile.

Yeah, sure, why not? replied Amar with a blush.

It has been just 5 days, and expectations are soaring high from Amar, said Mamta jokingly.

Of course they would be, Nischint said, while looking at Amar.

After this, Amar had lunch and took a nap. As he got up in the evening, the rest of the day ended quickly. He slept early, got up the next Monday morning, and the same schedule started again. He didn't have a lot of free time to think, time flew by, and all his worries and enigmas vanished. Finally, the first month is about to get completed in a couple of days. Initially, when Amar started teaching, he used to count days, but after a while, he never paid attention to that thing.

One day, after he finished teaching, Uncle Yamraaj handed over 2,000 rupees and said, Amar, I could see your efforts while you were teaching, and you truly deserved the amount.

Amar felt something different, and soon the feelings of excitement and success took over.He took it and said thank you to Uncle Yamraaj.

After this, he started his walk to the house. He was as excited as if he has just turned 12 and was returning home from school.

While moving quickly, he realised that Sanskriti had talked about having a mobile phone cover with his first salary.

"Should I be giving her a surprise by gifting it tomorrow?"

"Yeah, if you want to make it a surprise for her, then you can't tell anyone that you have received your first ever salary."

"Yeah. I could buy that for her and surprise everyone as well. Let's see what reaction they are going to give, but first I need to control my excitement and act normal as well."

After taking a deep breath, he entered the house, didn't talk much to anyone, and finished the day in his usual style. The next day, he left the house 30 minutes earlier than his usual time to buy the mobile phone cover for his sister. Once he bought the mobile cover, he reached his uncle's house without wasting any time. He was so eager to get home that he taught a bit less than his usual schedule. Once done with teaching, he quickly left for home.

As soon as he arrived , everyone was busy doing their own individual thing.

"Everyone, please come to the dinner's table," Amar yelled.

Everyone scrambled at the table, and when Mamta noticed Amar's excitement, she asked, What happened, Amar? Have you gotten a new job?

Well, mama, I haven't got a new job, but I have a surprise gift for Sanskriti, said Amar while giving the gift to Sanskriti.

Wow, a gift for me! said Sanskriti in excitement.

What's inside? asked Nischint as it was wrapped.

By the time Amar could say anything, Sanskriti shouted with joy, Yay! A brand new mobile cover for me.

I get it now why Amar is so happy and why he got this gift for Sanskriti, said Mamta.

Well, congratulations on your first salary, and keep going, said Nischint with pride.

After a few minutes of receiving congratulations from his family members, they finally took a selfie together to commemorate this special day.While going to his room after the selfie, Mamta suggested to Amar that he could buy himself a pair of new shoes with whatever money he has left. After nodding to her, he went to his room and marked today's date as one of his best days in his life.

The next day, he was preparing a few things to teach. He heard his phone ringing, and it was his friend Samridh on the call.

He quickly picked up the call and said, Hey, Samridh, How are you? It has been quite a while since we last spoke.

Yeah, I am alright. How about you? What have you been doing for the time being? asked Samridh.

Yeah, it has been the same and nothing new. How is your business going on? replied Amar.

Nothing going for now as things are still shaky, responded Samridh.

They kept talking for another 5 minutes before call ended, and Amar didn't tell him about his teaching stint because it was only for 2 months, out of which 1 month has just passed.

He again started his preparation and passed the rest of the day doing the usual things: teaching, getting home, having food, and sleep.

Finally, after a few more weeks of teaching, only one more week is left for the two months to be completed. He really liked this teaching job and wanted to continue it.

"Tomorrow is Sunday, and I must find some other students to continue this teaching job," said Amar to himself before heading out to his uncle's house.

He finished the day and went to sleep early to have good rest before he starts pondering about "how to find more students" on Sunday. Finally, Sunday morning has arrived. He is all set to start brainstorming after having breakfast. Winter mornings are ideal for enjoying clear blue skies and warm sunlight.

"How can I find more students to teach as I feel it is one of the best jobs in the world?"

After a while,

"I think I can print some pamphlets and distribute them in my community, and maybe install a small board about tuition classes in front of the house."

"Yeah, you can get pamphlets as well as a small board with the money you are about to get."

"Yeah, that is the right strategy, I believe."

"I think you are forgetting something. Something more important than getting new students or continuing this"

"That thing is always on my mind, and...

Amar heard his phone ringing. It was his friend, Samridh.

"I think he would be asking me about when I would be meeting him, but right now I am in no mood to get myself distracted."

Amar let the phone ring, and finally it stopped.

"I recall very clearly what is most important. It is just that I wasn't actively thinking about it. The idea I had in my mind to test the theory of the Samridh regarding how earning money brings more respect and human value in the family has been tested only once as of now, when I earned money for the first time. I could tell he was correct because everyone was extra nice to me when I got my first pay. I would have another chance to test it soon because I will be getting my second payout. If it gets proven correct this time, I would believe in it wholeheartedly. In fact, I could see that everyone is excited, and I haven't heard Mama and Papa talking about my job or my future worries. There is absolutely no discussion about it."

"Perhaps they do it in the evening when you are not present, as they used to do."

"I think I should try to hear what they are talking about me when I am not around. I will use the same trick as the one I used last time to hear them."

"Yeah, from tomorrow onwards, you may try and get it."

"Yes Perfect. Before I could see their reaction on my second payment, let's try to get what they are thinking about me now and how much that thinking has changed since I started making money."

After finding a new mission, Amar is off to take a nap since it is Sunday. He spent the rest of his evening in his room while watching videos and surfing internet. Finally, Monday is here. Amar has finished his teaching and is off to his house. As soon as he reached his house, he hid himself behind the window to see if there was any kind of discussion going on about him. He stayed there, but no discussion happened between his parents even after half an hour. As it started getting cold, Amar wished himself good luck for tomorrow while moving into the house.

"One day wasted," said Amar while entering his room.

Today is Tuesday, and Amar is all set with his position to hear some sort of discussion about him. He heard some discussion going on between his parents, but sadly, it was not about him, his future, or anything related to them.

"Better luck tomorrow," Amar said, and he walked into the house as it was quite cold outside.

Wednesday is here, and Amar is hoping to get lucky on third attempt. He arrived about 10 minutes earlier than his usual time to give himself an edge in his mission. He took a seat behind the window, hoping to hear something substantial. He initially had no success because there was nothing going on in the house. After a couple of minutes, he heard some noises, but sadly, it was from the TV.

As he was about to give up and go inside, the TV abruptly switched off, and all he could hear was his father, Nischint, asking Mamta, Is Amar home?

No, he hasn't gotten home, though he must be home by now, replied Mamta.

He might still be teaching and come home late, said Nischint .

I think I better give him a call to ask where he is and when will he be home, replied Mamta.

I suggest you don't disturb him now as he has started working, and let him enjoy his work.I could see that he is totally immersed in teaching, which is good, as enjoying what you do always keeps a person fresh and happy. suggested Nischint

Yeah, that is what I can feel by seeing how he has changed himself. Instead of spending a lot of time on his phone and in front of the computer, he's reading books to prepare lessons to teach, Mamta responded.

Yes, responsibilities do bring about strong changes in a person. I can see him becoming more responsible with time management now since he has started working and growing in life. After this short stint of 2 months of teaching, he should try to find something soon again to continue making money and eventually get his pay increased as well, Nischint suggested.

Yeah, that is what he would be trying as he got the experience of how hard it is to make money and how to spend it smartly, replied Mamta.

Yes, I believe so, and since two people are making money in the family now instead of one, my worries regarding the future are fended off very well, said Nischint.

Yeah, the constant worries we had about how he would start making his career are not that strong as he has started it somehow, and I am sure that even after the end of these two months, he won't sit for too long and will find other things to do to make money, replied Mamta.

Anyway, what are you cooking for dinner tonight? Nischint asked Mamta a question.

As soon as Amar heard it, he realised that what he wanted to hear was over and it was time to go in because it has been a while since he is out and shivering from the cold.

As he entered the house, Mamta asked him, How are you, Amar, and how was your teaching?

He replied only with an "Okay, Mama," and entered his room.

"It was odd that she didn't ask why I was late."

"Is it due to the fact that you have started making money and no longer a jobless guy?"

"Maybe, but right now it's better to change clothes and have some tea rather than putting my mind into other things. Maybe after dinner I can give it some thought."

"Yeah Alright"

After this, Amar enjoyed tea and later had dinner. Once he finished dinner, he was quickly off to bed and ready to give some thought to what had been on his mind earlier. As soon as he put a bit of stress on his mind, he fell asleep due to being extremely tired. He got up straight in the morning.

"Oh my gosh, I fell asleep last night so quickly that I didn't even remove my shocks."

He jumped out of bed, took a shower, and ate breakfast.

"Only 3 days are left for my 2 months of stint, and somehow I have found the answer to the most complex question, and I must admit that Samridh was spot on with his understanding about money and respect, at least. I can't say much about my parents making my life hard if i loose money in business, but I can say that my respect and value have surely gone up as I have started making money, though the amount is very small."

"Yeah, you are right. It was quite evident from Papa's yesterday statement versus the one he made before you started making money.His perception is changed quite a lot about you"

"Absolutely .Though they never discussed it with me to contribute financially but they had that thing on their mind always, and things could have been bad had I not started making money."

"Yes, based on Samridh experience, you would be confronted daily with the most common question of when you would start making money, and I believe that would have made your life hell."

"Yes, and since I have got my answer, I better find a few more students to teach after this to continue making money."

"Yes, and now no more discussion for the rest of the week."

After this, Amar made sure to give all his attention to teaching as only 3 days were left for the completion of 2 months.

Finally, it's the last day of teaching. Once he finished teaching the last day, Uncle Yamraaj, Aunt, and even Akshat said thank you to Amar for his dedicated teaching. Uncle Yamraaj gave him 2,000 rupees as his pay for this month, and he left in joy to reach his house.

While on the way, he thought about how to use this money.

"Well, as I have decided to continue teaching, I would spend this money to print some pamphlets and install a board about tuition classes in front of the house. Whatever would be left, I would use to buy something for Mummy and Papa."

With these thoughts in mind, Amar reached home. It's Saturday evening, and finally his mission of two months of teaching is done. He wants to relax and rest,that's why he didn't set the alarm for Sunday morning. Sunday morning has arrived, and Amar is awake at the same time he used to be due to the habit he developed over the course of two months. He felt very relaxed and calm, as he had achieved some great success with teaching in the past couple of months. He enjoyed a good breakfast followed by resting in the house garden with bright sunlight and a cool breeze. As he is enjoying the sunlight and feeling the warmth of it, he realises that Samridh called him on Sunday and he didn't pick it up.

"Let's call Samridh and indirectly thank him for his spot-on theory about earning money and respect going up in the family."

With this thought in his mind, he dialled Samridh.

After a few rings, Samridh finally picked up the call.

Hey Samridh,Good morning,How are you? asked Amar.

I am just fine, Amar, and how about you? replied Samridh.

I am good as well. I'm sorry, I was busy on Sunday and missed your call, Amar explained.

Yeah, I understand.Recently I had a minor loss in business, and it is still shaky and struggling to work, replied Samridh.

Oh . I am sorry to hear that, Samridh. I think once things get better, you will be able to recover this minor loss, said Amar, while showing empathy.

That's correct, but I can't tell my parents about it because they'll make my life even more difficult by asking when I'll be able to recover the money so i have to keep this thing within me, Samridh replied.

I think you are a bit harsh on your parents. You have been earning for so long, and profit and loss are part of business. If you explain things nicely to them, they would understand it as well, suggested Amar.

I understand your point of view as well, but I am sure they would not understand it , and as I have faced it before, I don't want to fall into that trap again, replied Samridh.

Okay, well, best of luck with your efforts to recover the loss, and I am confident you will be able to do so, Amar said while giving assurance.

Thank you for your support, Amar. I also hope to recover it soon, replied Samridh, and the call ended.

"I understand that initially, when he started business, he made some loss, which made his parents furious about it, but surely now they won't be that harsh on him as he has been making money for years and is financially independent now."

"Yeah, that's right, but remember, you doubted his money and respect theory, which ended up being true, and if he is speaking this, there might be some truth behind it."

"I still won't believe that if he ended up losing some money in the business he started, they would go on to rebuke him for that."

"Yes, that sounds logical, but who knows? He might be right as well."

"Who knows, he could be right, but I can't test this theory because I haven't had any business losses and I don't have any money to invest in any business. Even if I had incurred a loss, I don't think Mom and Dad would be that harsh on me. They might discuss it between them, but surely they won't be that harsh on me regarding that."

"I can't say anything about it since I was totally wrong previously about earning money and respect, so it's better for you, Amar, not to rely on any speculation made in the air."

"Yeah, and unfortunately, I can't test this theory, so I'll never know how Mom and Papa would have reacted."

"Yes absolutely."

After this, Amar didn't think much about it, as he was not in the mood to feel stressed. He enjoyed the rest of the day, enjoying good food and the cool weather. In the evening, when Nischint arrived, he looked a bit tense.

Mamta asked, What happened, Nischint? You look worried.

The entire day was a drama, Nischint responded.

Please don't make riddles for us, Papa. Tell us what happened, Amar suggested.

You know my friend, Mr. Ram Sagar. His son invested in some online thing and lost money in that, due to which , he was scolding him a lot on the phone whole day , replied Nischint.

What online thing did he lose the money in, and how much? Amar inquired with a shock.

Something called Crypto, or what is it called? Bitcoin, or something like that, and yeah, he lost 5,000 rupees, replied Nischint.

Papa, that is called crypto, or virtual currency. I think Uncle Ram Sagar overreacted, as 5000 is not a big amount to scold so harshly. I know his son very well, as he was my junior in the school. He's a very smart guy; maybe this is the first time he's invested money and lost it, Amar lamented.

Amar, you worked so hard for two months to make 4,000, and here this guy loses 5,000 all at once. His father works tirelessly to earn every penny, and his son should have given it some thought before investing, and if there was even 1% of risk, he should have backed out, Nischint responded with abysmal.

Yeah, Papa, I understand your point, and I am not denying it, but anyone could make a mistake, and I am sure Ram Sagar uncle could have discussed it with him in private rather than making it a public issue, said Amar.

Before this conversation could move towards an argument, Sanskriti stepped in and said,

I think both are at fault. His son can't be ignorant of the fact that he is old enough to understand the financial condition of his house, and he should have consulted someone before making an investment. Since he has made a mistake, Uncle Ram Sagar needed to understand that his son has made a mistake, and they could have solved this thing within the family rather than making it an issue at work.

I think Sanskriti is absolutely right, said Mamta.

Even after an excellent explanation, both Amar and his father did not agree with the statement and had their opinions exactly different from each other, as the father was siding with another father and the son was showing his defence with his school junior.

After this short, unexpected burst of thinking, Amar quickly had his dinner and went off to bed.

"The entire day was going great, but sadly, the minor argument with Papa has ruined the entire mood."

"While the argument was there, something else also happened there, if you have noticed."

"I was so focused on the other things that I might have totally missed it."

"The intensity Papa was using to defend Uncle Ram Sagar's behaviour and scolding towards his son, and that too for 5000 rupees, though you also know how brilliant his son is."

"Yeah, and if I'm not mistaken, he's been giving tuition classes to many students for nearly two years, and it would take less than a month to recover that money. It's not that I'm completely blind and don't understand or see Uncle Ram Sagar's effort to make money, and since

I've worked for 2 months as well, I understand how difficult it is to make money, but instead of getting hyper,understanding things and solving them calmly is the only way to make things better, because yelling and scolding won't bring his son's money back, but it will certainly make his son further depressed."

"I believe Samridh was correct in his assessment that his parents will severely reprimand him if he tells them about his business loss, as evidenced by Uncle Ram Sagar's behaviour."

"If a 5000 rupee loss could make Uncle Ram Sagar that angry, imagine Samridh parents knowing about his loss, and the sad part is that both are working and making money as well."

"Imagine if you invested in business with Samridh and ended up losing money, you would get a good thrashing from parents as well and daily all-day lectures about how wrong you were."

"Earlier I might not have believed in it, but now I think Samridh might be right that even my parents, who have been very patient and calm with me, could turn belligerent towards me after knowing that I have incurred losses. Luckily, I have no money to invest, but sadly, I can never get to know their reaction.I wish there was a way to find out, but there isn't."

"Yes, that's true, and I believe you should focus on finding some students so that you can continue making money."

"Yeah, it's late night now. I'll think about what to print on pamphlets and board tomorrow."

Amar dozed off and woke up the next morning.

"Today I need to get the design for pamphlets done and maybe the design for the board as well. I don't want to waste time at all."

After this, he quickly left the bed and got done with breakfast.

As he was about to turn on his computer, suddenly Mamta asked him, Amar, are you busy now?

I'm not that occupied, mama. Why?,replied Amar.

Well, since you were busy teaching for a couple of months, no one deposited the money in the bank. If you're free now, you could go get it deposited, Mamta suggested.

Of course, why not? It's been a long time since I've been in the bank, Amar replied.

He took money from his mother and left the house to get to the bank. He deposited the money quickly in the bank, and while coming back, he passed by the park where he used to go.

"The bank deposit didn't take long, and I could visit the park for a while to see how it is now."

As he entered the park, he saw new benches being installed with new blooming flowers. He sat down on a newly installed bench and started thinking about what to print on pamphlets .Suddenly his phone rang, and it was his friend Samridh.

He quickly picked up the phone and said, Hey, Samridh. How are you, my friend?

I am just fine, and how about you? asked Samridh.

I am okay as well and enjoying the warm sunlight in the park, replied Amar.

You are enjoying the sun, whereas I am facing the heat now as your suggestion totally backfired, said Samridh with disappointment.

Which suggestion are you referring to? Amar inquired, surprised.

I took your advice to share with my parents about the minor loss I had, and now they are judging me for failed business management. Samridh responded.

I'm sorry to hear that, Samridh. I was hoping that sharing that minor loss news with them would bring you some relief, but unfortunately it opened a Pandora's box for you, Amar replied.

Yeah, it did, but it was not surprising for me as I knew it was going to happen, but I tested it just to see how they would behave, and they did exactly what I predicted, said Samridh.

Yeah, and I hope that you recover that loss soon to get rid of that heat, suggested Amar.

Yeah, thank you, Amar. I also suggest you wait to get into business until you have your own money. At the very least, if you lose it, you won't feel the heat from your parents, Samridh said.

Yeah, I understand it now, replied Amar before hanging up the phone.

"I have two strong cases in front of me where parents are going crazy after their children for minor losses in life. It seems like money has taken over human values for sure, even in family."

After a couple of minutes of thinking,

"Well, it has been over half an hour since I got into this park, and I better get out of here as initially I decided to be here for a while"

As he is moving towards his house, money and human values involving families have taken up a firm position in his mind. It is so firm that even things like finding new students to teach have taken a backseat in his mind. He wants to know what his parents would do if he suffered a loss. Are they going to act the same way as Samridh's parents or become like Uncle Ram Sagar? Would they encourage him to work hard and recover from his loss, or would they condemn him harshly? By the time he reached the house, lunch was ready. He had it and took a nap to calm his mind down. He started his evening with tea and some snacks.

One more Test please!

"Is there a way I could test my parents without even incurring any loss?"

"How is it even possible? When you don't have money to invest, how could you end up losing any amount? It appears that you must fake it until you make it. Like you lie to Mummy and Papa about losing money on an investment and keep telling them until you get their reaction. Actually, it's a good idea, and no actual loss would be incurred as well."

"What? You mean I should lie to them and say I have lost money in business and see how they react? It sounds fascinating, but it's not practical because they would catch me lying, and if they found out, it could tarnish my image and cost me respect in their eyes."

"You can always tell them the truth at any moment if you feel things are getting out of control."

"It is worth a try, but there are high chances that either I will get caught or things won't be nice ever after that."

"To get something, we need to take risks and sometimes make sacrifices as well.You can always explain to them why you decided to conduct this experiment with full honesty if you get caught or when it gets over"

"I need to plan it very well. It can't be done overnight. I need to understand the risks associated with it. I need to take it as an experiment where there will be a strong reaction and it can fail as well."

"Yes, a foolproof plan is needed, and maybe some strong preparation is also needed to make it as genuine as possible."

Amar didn't realise it was late at night and dinner was ready. He rushes into his room after finishing dinner.

"I think I have some ideas for how to play this. I don't have any money to invest, and even if I did, I wouldn't know where to put it because I know nothing about investing. So, in order to elicit genuine reactions from parents, I must fake the loss and do so in such a way that it appears completely genuine. I better write things down on a paper to make sure things go according to plan."

Amar took out a page from his notebook and wrote "The Family Experiment" on the top of it.

"How long should this experiment last? 2 days or more."

"I think 2 days are a very short time period. I am sure it would take them about 2–3 days to get serious about it, as at first they would take it as a joke. 10 days seem ideal because it takes 2-3 days for them to become serious, and then rest 7-8 days to see how they react.You can plan it for 10 days at first, but keep the option to cancel if things get out of hand. Don't go beyond 10 days because each passing day will be difficult for you."

Now Amar has written 10 days in the duration column on the page.

"How much money should I tell them that I lost?"

"You could tell them anything because you are just faking it."

"I think I should use the exact amount I have in my bank account, which are saved by Mama and Papa."

"Yes, as that account belongs to you, you can withdraw it and hide it somewhere in the form of cash to make the loss as genuine as possible, as once you tell them that you have lost it, they will definitely try to access your bank account to see the balance."

"So it means I am going to tell them that I have lost as much as 500k Indian rupees. That is insane."

"Unfortunately, you have to tell them this big amount, as with a smaller amount, they might not show true reactions and discuss it in your absence."

Now, Amar has written the amount as 500k rupees in the loss column on the paper.

"Now I have the amount and the idea how to hide it. How about when they would ask me, Where did I lose it?"

"The reason must be very practical, as you can't tell them you invested with Samridh. The moment you tell them, they will surely ask Samridh, and he will spill the truth that you never invested with him. Remember what Papa said a few days ago about Ram Sagar Uncle's son? You could use the same reason, and as it happened in reality, things would totally appear genuine."

"Yes, I could use that crypto currency reason, and it would totally appear genuine."

Amar stated the reason for the loss as "Crpyto currency investment" on the paper.

"Now I have the amount, the reason, and the days. What I am left with is when to start it and what preparation I needed to do to make it happen."

At this Moment, Amar looked at the wall clock, which has just ticked over 1 a.m.

"I better sleep now, and tomorrow I'm going to find answers to a few questions I have in mind."

He quickly turned off his room light before falling asleep. When he awoke the next morning, the first thing that came into his mind was finding answers to the remaining questions for the experiment. It seems like that experiment has clearly taken over his mind, and things are not going to get better unless he finds answers and gets done with it. He quickly finished his breakfast and went off to his room . He didn't pay any attention to the weather or what was going on in his house.

"What kind of preparation do I need and when should I be starting it?"

"The first thing is that, you avoid talking much to the family members, which would give them the impression that you are having anxiety about something. Reduce food and sleep intake so that anxiety would be visible on the face as well."

"How about when should I start it off?"

"I think you can take the next 15 days to prepare for it and start it off on the 2nd of April to avoid any confusion with April Fool's Day. It would also be simple for you to count the days from 2nd April."

"So the initial planned duration would be from April 2nd to April 11th."

Then Amar mentioned it on the sheet of paper.

As he was going further with his planning then suddenly Mamta appeared in his room.

Amar, what happened to you? You have been very preoccupied for the past couple of days. What is your new mission?

Nothing, Mama, just thinking about what to do next as my stint of teaching is over, replied Amar.

If you like teaching, you may try to find a few more students to give them home tuition, suggested Mamta.

Yeah, I am thinking about it.I may print some pamphlets and even install a board outside the house to inform people that I am teaching students, replied Amar.

See, you have the idea of how to find students, but still you look so worried, said Mamta curiously.

I am a bit worried about the design of those pamphlets as well as the board I want to install, replied Amar.

That is not a big thing, Amar, as you can take Sanskriti's help, as she is very good with creativity and designing, suggested Mamta.

Yeah, I would ask her to suggest me a few designs, replied Amar.

Don't be stressed about things, whether they are small or big, as over time if you keep working hard, they will get resolved, said Mamta while petting his shoulder.

Mamta asked Amar to have his lunch because it was already afternoon, which he obviously didn't realise. After finishing off his lunch, he tried to take a nap but couldn't sleep as things were getting intense in his mind.

"I think I need to stop thinking about other things and try to complete this experiment to settle it once and for all. I will start doing things tomorrow.The first thing I need to do is withdraw saving from my bank account and stash them somewhere safe."

"I think it's somewhere no one would expect it to be, and it stays safe there."

"Yeah, I got it. I am going to hide them inside my pillow, and that is the only place I can think off where no one would expect or try to search for them. By tomorrow, I would have finished withdrawing money and hidden it safely. I do things one at a time, so there would be very little chance of a mistake or something going wrong."

As he was planning things further, he suddenly heard a knock on his door.

Who is there? asked Amar.

It's me, Sanskriti.

Give me a minute, Amar said as he approached the door to open it.

As she walked into the room, Amar asked her, "What happened?"

Nothing, Bhaiya (brother), Mama told me that you need assistance with tuition pamphlets and board design, Sanskriti replied.

Yeah, I remember it. I want you to help me design a pamphlet and maybe a board regarding tuition classes, said Amar.

Okay, Bhaiya (brother), let me use your computer and show you some designs, replied Sanskriti.

Amar sat next to her as she started making some designs on it.

As the process would take some time, Amar inquired, How is your school going on Sanskriti?

It is going well, and I think since you have suggested to Mama and Papa that I attend an art college, I could see myself becoming a successful artist. In fact, I have shared it with my teachers at school, and even they have suggested that I join an art college to further sharpen my artistic skills, replied Sanskriti.

Yeah, I have the same feeling. As you can see, every single family is dreaming off to make their children doctors, scientists, or engineers, which is definitely not possible. A lot of times they want to opt for careers in other fields like artistry or sports, but due to family pressure, they end up taking something they have no interest in and failing very badly at it, said Amar.

Yes, Bhaiya (brother), that is very true, and I am always grateful to you that you saved me from that vicious loop of doing things that I am not interested in, replied Sanskriti.

Yeah, that's my responsibility as a brother to keep you out of trouble, Amar said lovingly.

As soon as Amar finished speaking, Sanskriti said, Look, Bhaiya(brother), I have created this design for Pamphlets.

Once Amar looked at it, he was amazed by the creativity of Sanskriti, as it looked perfect.

Wow! That looks so amazing. I liked the way you have shown students learning with "Nice Tuition Classes" written in bold letters, said Amar.

Do you want me to change anything like font or colour? asked Sanskriti.

Nah, everything is perfect, and how about the board, which I want to install outside the house? replied Amar.

I will make it tomorrow, as I am not getting the idea for it now, and I need some more time for it, Bhaiya(brother), said Sanskriti.

Yeah, take your time and give your best. I think my suggestion to join you the art college is not going to fail for sure after seeing your lovely creativity for these pamphlets, replied Amar with a laugh.

Yeah, trust me, I can deliver much better than your expectations, said Sanskriti while going out with a chuckle.

Once she left, Amar realised that, after such a long time, he had a wonderful conversation with Sanskriti.

"When we were young, we used to converse a lot in the evening, but now things have changed a lot. I was in such a rush to plan things for that experiment that I couldn't keep my mind at peace, but a lovely conversation with her helped me to calm my mind down."

"I don't believe you need to rush or try to plan too many things at once. You have enough time to do things one by one."

"Yes, so I will focus on tomorrow. I will go to the bank and get that thing done, then I will see what things are left to be done after that."

Amar, dinner is ready. Where are you? Amar heard his father asking him.

Yes, I am in my room, Papa, and give me two minutes.I will be there, replied Amar.

Once Amar got there to join them, everyone was waiting for him.

What happened to you, Amar? Your mama is saying that for the past few days, you have spent too much time in your room. Is everything all right with you? Nischint asked as soon as he sat down.

Yeah, papa, everything is alright. I was struggling to get the design for pamphlets, but Sanskriti has helped me with that, replied Amar.

Yeah, so your main concern is solved now, so don't keep yourself in your room, Mamta advised.

Okay, mama, I will try not to be locked inside and let's eat food as dinner is getting cold now, suggested Amar.

They all finished dinner, and Amar decided not to think anything further and went to sleep because he knew what to do tomorrow.

He rushed through his shower and breakfast the next morning. He is all set to start off the most important part of the experiment. As he was about to get out of the house to get to the bank, he was heckled by Mamta, who asked him, Where are you going today, Amar?

He wasn't prepared to answer and obviously can't speak the truth as well. Suddenly he remembered about that pamphlet design and replied, Mama, I am going to find a printing service to get my pamphlets printed and get a quotation for my board as well.

Okay, that's fine, Amar.Be back on time, as I have made your favourite Shahi Paneer, said Mamta.

Okay, I will be back by lunch, replied Amar as he left the house.

"I better quickly go to the bank to withdraw the money and get straight to house as it is risky to be out with such a huge amount of cash."

He quickly got to the bank, and when he inquired about withdrawing the amount, he was informed that any amount that big can only be withdrawn with prior request, and if he made the request now by tomorrow morning, he could get it. After making the request, Amar is out of the bank.

"It has been only an hour, and I can't go back to the house now, as Mom would doubt how I could be back so early. I need to spend at least one more hour outside before I can return to the house."

"What can you do in the next hour to pass the time?"

"Well, I could visit some printing service and see what they charge me for board and pamphlets."

After walking for a while, Amar saw a printing service shop. He went there to make some inquiries about board and pamphlet printing.

After receiving a quote, Amar decided to print only 50 pamphlets because board was too expensive for his current budget. The printing service told him that by tomorrow he could collect his printed pamphlets.

"This is perfect, as I could collect money and pamphlets together."

"Wow, time is flying at a rapid rate," said Amar after realising that it has been almost 50 minutes since he finished his bank work.

"I think if I start walking towards house, by the time I get home, it will be perfect lunch time."

His calculation came just in time, as he reached home exactly during lunch time.

Mamta asked him ,what happened to your pamphlets as soon as he arrived.Yeah, I have ordered them, and I will get them tomorrow morning, replied Amar.

Okay, that's good. Here's your Favourite Shahi Paneer and Rice.

I miss my favourite Shahi Paneer and Rice. Thanks, Mama, for making it for me, replied Amar while taking his first bite.

After having lunch, he took a nap, as his mind was very calm due to the fact that he knew exactly what to do tomorrow morning. He spent the evening watching television because he didn't want to think about anything. Finally, next morning is here, and Amar is all set to take the first step after a false start yesterday. As he was about to leave the house, he said, I am going out, mom, to get those pamphlets I gave to print yesterday. "Okay" is what Mamta replied in return. As he got out of the house, he headed straight to the bank.

"I better collect pamphlets first, then go to the bank, as it is not safe to walk around ."

Amar went to pick up his pamphlets and was pleased with the print quality. He asked for a bigger poly bag so that he could carry the cash in that bag as well. After this, he quickly went to the bank to get the withdrawal and kept cash in the bottom of the bag and put pamphlets on top to avoid any suspicion. He quickly rushed to the house, and as soon as he reached it, he almost bumped into Sanskriti.

As she saw him carrying a big bag, she asked, Bhaiya (brother), what's inside this big bag?

There are the pamphlets. I ordered them yesterday, and today they are ready, replied Amar.

May I see them, Bhaiya (brother)? asked Sanskiti.

Yeah sure. Call mama also. I will show both of you together, answered Amar nervously.

As Sanskriti moved from there to find Mamta, Amar quickly took the money and put it into his pillow. After this, he showed pamphlets to both Mamta and Sanskriti. Sanskriti even took 20 of them to distribute in the nearby locality.

They look absolutely amazing, Amar, and what a good design by Sanskriti, said Mamta.

Both Amar and Sanskriti said "thank you" to her.Amar breathed a sigh of relief after successfully concealing the cash in his pillow.

"Finally, the first step is done, and luckily, no one raised any suspicion about it. I hope no one looks into my pillow until this experiment gets over. Let's take some rest, as I don't have anything to do right now. Whatever steps are left, I will think about them at night."

By the time he got up in the evening, it was quite late.

"I slept for 4 hours rather than 2 hours, and the evening is almost over.Let's have an early dinner so I can plan my next steps."

As Amar went out of his room to get an idea of what was being cooked for dinner, he was surprised to see that his mother had not yet begun cooking. He looked for her and could not find her.

He asked Sanskriti, Where is mom?

Mom and Dad have gone outside for some work. They must be getting home soon, as they told me that they would be back in a couple of hours, replied Sanskriti.

As Amar wanted to ask his second question, right at that moment, the doorbell rang.

I think they are back, said Sanskriti while moving towards the door to open it.

As his parents walked in, he noticed that they are carrying two big bags.

What are these, and where did you go? asked Amar with some surprise.

Today I decided to give your mom a break from cooking dinner, so I went out with her to buy dinner from outside, and we bought some groceries for the house as well, said Nischint with excitement.

Yeah, that's half the truth. The rest of the truth is that we wanted to give a small treat to you and Sanskriti, added Mamta.

Treat for me . For what? asked Amar, with a shocked look on his face.

Well, you have recently completed two months of work, even Yamraaj uncle called me and praised the hard work and dedication you put in, replied Nischint.

And I showed those pamphlets to Papa, and he was so impressed with the design that it's a treat for Sanskriti as well, Mamta further said.

Well, that is so amazing. I am truly surprised. "Thank you, mom and dad," said Amar.

I think it's enough of a conversation, and let's have dinner as it's getting cold, suggested Mamta.

They all enjoyed a delicious dinner that had not been prepared at home in a long time. After dinner, Amar is in his room now and ready to plan his next steps.

As he gets ready to think further, he pays attention to what his inner soul is suggesting him.

"Do I really need this experiment to see how would they react me if I end up having some loss? I highly doubt that they would even criticise me after knowing that I lost money on investments. Yes, look at all of them. Mama made my favourite dish yesterday. Sanskriti designed and distributed some pamphlets. Even today, Mom and Dad bought food to treat me."

"That's correct, but human emotions can swing from good to bad to worse, and this experiment will also show you how they support you when you are at your lowest due to losing money."

"Yeah, and I am sure they would understand my condition and go out of their way to try their best to lift me up."

"What if they genuinely think that you have lost money and try their best to help you out, and in the end they get to know it was a lie?Knowing that it was an experiment would make them more furious than actually losing money."

"Yeah, that is my concern as well, and I need to find a solution for it. Maybe I would even find it hard to face them while telling the truth. It is going to be a wild swing of emotions for them. From knowing about the loss to knowing that it was a lie just to test their reactions "

"Yeah, I have got a solution, though it's not very clever.You should write an apology letter in which you explain why you decided to carry experiment, apologise for bothering them, explain where the money is, and make a big promise to never do something like this again."

"Yeah, I think that is a better idea, where I could simply hand over the letter to them and they could read and understand the whole situation rather than facing and explaining them."

"Yes, and further, you could apologise in person as well after they get done reading that letter."

"Now I know what is the next step I should take. Tomorrow I will take the whole day to write that apology letter and get it done."

"And you could keep that apology letter hidden with the cash, so just in case if they discover it, they won't think that you have robbed them and hid the money into your pillow."

"Yes, and it's past 1 a.m. now, so I should get some sleep."

The next morning is here, and Amar is all set to write the letter.

"What more should I write in that, apart from why I took this decision and where is the money?"

"I think you should appreciate them for their patience and support they are going to provide you even after knowing that you end up losing money."

After thinking a while, Amar is ready to write the letter. He has chosen a fairly long white page to write it on, as he strongly believes that there will be a lot of things to say.

"Dear Mom and Dad, I know you are extremely hurt by the news that I ended up losing 500k rupees in the form of investment. I am touched by your behaviour and the support you have provided me in this hard time. Even though I have lost money, you are still rooting for me and believing that I will be able to recoup it. I even appreciate Sanskriti's support despite knowing that this loss has put her art college plan at jeopardy.

Firstly, I would like to sincerely apologise for lying to you all and telling that I lost the money in crypto investment, but the truth is that they are safe with me, and I have hidden them into my pillow in my room.

Now you all would be thinking, Why did I lie about money and waited this long to tell you the truth?

The answer lies in the environment I was facing. I could see things happening around me that made me question my beliefs about human values, respect, and money. As I am growing, I can feel that respect and human values are getting weaker. Money and earning more and more money tend to pull respect and human values up. I was clearly thinking about what your reaction would be if you find out that I have lost the large saving we had set aside for Sanskriti's higher education.

I thought a lot about it before proceeding, as I could see even before this , throughout my life, you have all been very supportive to me and have always stood by my side. I still chose to proceed with it as my mind couldn't settle or be ready to believe what I witnessed happening in the outside world versus the world I have formed through you all. I want to settle it for once and all. Though it has troubled you all a lot, it has fully restored my faith in family and human values, and your behaviour has proven that money is important but it can never set the love and respect we have in our family apart.

Since I could see happiness on your faces since I started teaching, I would further give my best to find students and try to pursue a career in the teaching world. I promise you that I will never lie again and disturb you like this. I am truly satisfied with the love and care I have in the family."

Your obedient Son,

Amar.

"It took a while to write, but finally it is done."

"I think you have written it very well, and it is well compiled. Well done, Amar. If you were not seeking a career in teaching, you could have become a writer."

"Let's hide this letter where cash is hidden."

After a few seconds of self-promotion, Amar hid the letter where the cash was hidden. As he looked at the clock, it was almost 1 p.m.

"Lunch must be ready. Let's go out and see how things are going."

As he was about to move out of his room, Mama shouted, Amar, Amar, lunch is ready, to which he responded, I am coming there, Mama.

While having lunch, Sanskriti informed him that she has distributed those 20 pamphlets in the nearby locality.

Once Amar is done with lunch, he is back in his room.

"I have completed the two most important steps to initiate this experiment, and now all I need to do is wait till 2nd April to finally break the news. There might be a few small steps I need to take, but I can think about them after having my dinner. Let's have a short nap, as writing that letter has mentally drained me completely."

When Amar awoke from his nap, he has a severe headache.

"I think that letter is still showing its impact on my brain.I better have some tea now to dampen it."

He walked out and asked his mom, "Could you please make tea for me as I am having a severe headache?"

Yeah, beta (son) for sure, Mamta replied, and then she said, Could you please bring the headache medicine that I gave you last night, Sanskriti?

She came rushing in and said, Who needs it?

I am having a headache now, and that is why Mama called you to get this headache medicine, Amar replied.

Okay, bhaiya (brother), You go to your room and relax. I bring in medicine and a glass of water for you, replied Sanskriti.

While you are coming in, get me a cup of tea that mom is making now as well,requested Amar.

Yes, sure, I will bring it too.Now you go and have a rest in bed, replied Sanskriti.

Once Amar had the medicine, followed by Excellent Tea, he laid down in the bed. After a couple of hours, he was asked by Sanskriti for dinner, but he refused to have it. He eventually fell asleep and awoke at 3 a.m., early in the morning.

"Finally that headache is over and I can breathe freely now, but sadly I was supposed to plan the next few things."

"Well, you could plan them now as you have good rest and not feeling sleepy at all."

"Yeah, even though I feel that I missed the opportunity to plan things, there is not much left to be planned."

"Yeah, two big things are done successfully, and now you only need to wait to break the news with the appearance that you are tensed and having anxiety.Moreover, I think that Mom and Dad are getting some inkling that you are anxious about something due to the fact that you are spending much of your time in your room."

"It is a blessing in disguise, as I am planning my things and they are assuming that I am anxious about something which I really want them to believe."

"Things are looking good to carry out the experiment you want to have, and soon these waiting days will be over as well. I still doubt that you need that experiment, Amar. Things are okay now, and might go in a different direction once they realise it was only an experiment."

"If they would support and stand by my side after knowing that I have lost the years of saving, then surely they would understand and stand by my side even after knowing that it was a lie and why I went for the experiment. Should I cut the waiting time and break the news earlier than the planned date?"

"Why do you want to do that?"

"See, I worked really hard to plan these things, and I have already taken two big steps, so there's no going back.As I wait more and more, the fight in my mind regarding whether to go for it or not will keep happening until the news is broken to them."

"Yeah, but don't rush for that as you need some time to set the stage properly to break that news and make it look as genuine as possible. Since you need to give the impression of being anxious and busy, you better start reading articles online to increase your knowledge about many subjects, which would help you to teach students as you have decided to get into teaching.This way, you could increase your knowledge as well as have enough time to prepare for the experiment."

"Yeah, from today , I would start working on it, and I hope my mind stops hopping around the idea of needing this experiment or not."

After this idea was forged in his mind, Amar slept quickly, as there was not much of the night left to sleep. He got up with a clear plan in mind. finished off his morning routine followed by a lovely breakfast, and he has locked himself in and started reading a lot of things related to high school. After a couple of hours of reading, he understood a few important topics from high school.

"When I was in high school, I always felt scared of these topics and never tried to study them with concentration. Today, after so many years, I finished them in a couple of hours . If I had this level of focus in high school and beyond, I could have been the class topper."

Suddenly his phone started ringing, and it was Samridh on the call.

Hey Samridh, what's up? How are you?

I am okay,how about you? Replied Samridh.

You sound so happy. What happened? asked Amar with curiosity.

Yeah, and the reason for my happiness is that I would be able to recover the loss by the 10th of next month, and finally my parents would stop hammering me down, replied Samridh.

That is awesome, said Amar with excitement.

Yeah, it has been such a hard time for me, and finally I will be getting rid of it. Since I was really anxious about things, I wanted to get my mind to relax by going on a 2-3 day staycation to a nearby location. How about you? How are things going for you? asked Samridh.

Well, I have decided to teach high school students through tuition classes, and even distributed some pamphlets in a nearby locality to advertise myself, replied Amar.

Yeah, that's a good career start. I will try to get you some students as well. So are you free after the 10th of next month? Asked Samridh.

How about after 15th? Amar asked in response.

Yeah, any date of next month is fine. We may meet after the 10th to decide where to go and other things, suggested Samridh.

Yeah, we can meet on the 13th of next month to plan out the staycation and other things, replied Amar.

That is perfect, said Samridh while hanging up the call.

"That's almost perfect . I'll finish the experiment on 11th April , rest on 12th April , meet him on 13th April , have a staycation by 15th April , and relax my mind."

"Yeah, and after your staycation, you can start off your home tuition journey as well."

Amar, lunch is ready, said Mamta.

Yes, mama, I am coming.

"Wow, time is flying by at such a rapid rate that even the afternoon is here."

As Amar reached the dinner table, Sanskriti asked him, Bhaiya (brother), have you distributed the remaining 30 pamphlets?

No, I haven't, as I was busy with my own things, responded Amar.

I can distribute the remaining 30 for you if you want, offered Sanskriti.

Yeah, why not? After lunch, take those remaining 30 pamphlets and get them distributed. Thank you for your lovely service , replied Amar with a laugh.

Amar handed her the remaining pamphlets before starting his study of high school topics again.

"Now I can concentrate on my learning for the remaining days as I don't have any work in hand."

"Hopefully, by the time your experiment ends, you will get a few students to start off your teaching journey."

Amar continued studying the whole evening in his room before making his last appearance in front of his family at the dinner table. He even reduced the dinner amount to give the impression that he was anxious about something. He continued this same pattern of getting up in the morning, having breakfast, then being inside the room until lunch was ready, then again studying, followed by dinner. His family initially failed to pick up the changes in his eating pattern, and the days keep passing by. Finally, April 1st has arrived. Everyone is home today, including Nischint and Sanskriti due to a public holiday.

Amar got up and followed the same pattern he has been following for many days. As he started his day today, Nischint noticed that Amar had left one chapati (wheat tortilla) on his breakfast plate.

He quickly asked Mamta, What happened to Amar? Is he eating less nowadays?

Yeah, I noticed that he has been eating less for the past couple of days and is usually in his room the whole day. He only comes out to eat, and that's it , Mamta replied with a worried face.

Didn't you ask him if there was anything bothering him? asked Nischint.

Yeah, I tried to ask him previously, but he seems to usually avoid that question, and his replies are often very short in the "Okay" form," replied Mamta.

I think we should talk to him and ask him if he is under tension or stress about something. Staying in the room the whole day, eating less suddenly, and avoiding the question after being asked what's going on in his life are not good signs. He could be facing something serious, and keeping it to himself won't help him either, said Nischint.

Yeah, I do understand your concern as well. Should we go now and talk to him about what he is hiding? asked Mamta.

I think now it is not the right time, as we are all going to have lunch soon. We go to his room in the evening with Sanskriti and try to ask him what he is hiding and resolve any issue he is facing. One more thing I would like to mention is that you don't ask him anything when we have lunch in a while. Just stay normal and let's see if he eats less or not, and even if he does, don't point it out at that moment. We will ask him and discuss all these hings with him in the evening .Okay?, said Nischint.

"Yeah, that is the right approach, I believe, and even if we have to coax him a bit, we would do it to get the truth out of him, but in the evening, replied Mamta.

Yeah, and let's call him for lunch, as we need to take some rest after lunch as well, said Nischint.

They all had lunch after this, and as usual, Amar ate less food and walked back to his room. This thing further worried both Nischint and Mamta, but as they had decided to have their sweet interrogation with Amar in the evening and they went to take a nap. On the other side, Amar, unknown to this development, stuck to his laptop, reading a few more topics left in the whole high school syllabus. After reading for another hour, he has finally studied and understood every single topic in high school.

"Today is the last day of my wait, and luckily, I have even finished off the last few topics as well."

"From tomorrow onwards, you are going to have a complete turn around, and it is going to last for a little over a week before things calm down and you meet with Samridh."

"Earlier, I felt that I couldn't wait for 2nd April to start off the experiment, and now I can't wait to finish it off as I can already predict the result."

"Wait is almost over, high school topics are done, and you have nothing else to do now, so let's take a nap before you finish off this evening."

It's evening now, and all family members have scrambled themselves to walk into Amar's house, though he is still sleeping in peace, unaware of what is coming. They knocked on his door, which finally broke his nap. All he could hear was his parents knocking on the door and asking him to open the door. As he opened the door, they all entered in. Amar was in a state of shock as he saw them there together.

What happened. Is everything alright, Mom, Dad, and Sanskriti? asked Amar with a perplexed face.

That is what we are here to ask you. Is everything alright? What is happening with you? Are you in any trouble or having problem, beta (son)? Mamta asked him.

Yeah, I am okay, and there is nothing going on, Amar responded with a shaky voice.

Then why are you locked in your room the whole day? You have even reduced your food and cut the talking time as well, said Nischint while showing concern.

Don't say it's because you're worried about the designs of the pamphlets or board , because Sanskriti has assisted you in both designing and distributing them, Mamta said.

I think it's best to tell us the truth, Bhaiya (brother), and maybe we could help you with that, said Sanskriti as well.

Amar was not expecting it to happen, more so with the number of questions thrown at him. He started feeling nervous with his lips dried. He took a few sips of water and calmed himself down. They could also see him struggling to respond because he is completely frozen in time.

How long are we supposed to wait before you can explain to us what is going on with you? What trouble are you in? Nischint said to Amar.

By now Mamta has realised that surely he is hiding something, as he has been shaky in his behaviour and has failed to maintain eye contact.

Amar, it is evidently clear that you are hiding something, and we are here to know it. We understand that you might not be in the right condition to speak about it right now, but we are also worried for you. We don't want to force you to tell us now, but if you could please tell us by tomorrow what you have been hiding so that we could help you, even if we can't help you directly, we will stand by your side, said Mamta with a worrisome look.

I think your health is not Okay now, Bhaiya (brother), so please take some rest now, and if you need anything to eat, just ask us. We better go out now, mom and dad, and I'm confident that Amar Bhaiya (brother) will not disappoint us and will reveal what he is keeping away from us tomorrow. Amar Bhaiya (brother), Mom and Dad are extremely worried for you, and I hope once you tell them the thing you have been hiding for a while, it will ease their worries a lot, said Sanskriti before they all move out.

As they leave his room now, Amar lies in bed without even saying a single word to them.

"Today it was a very emotional and heartbreaking moment as they all came here to ask me what was wrong with me. It will be even more difficult for me to remain in the experiment once I break the news and allow it to begin from tomorrow. I hope these 10 days pass quickly and I get positive results from this Family Experiment that I have planned. I better sleep now as tomorrow could be a long day for all of us."

Action is about to start!

Finally, the 2nd of April is here, and Amar is up in the morning. He is really nervous and anxious about how he is going to break the news.

"I think i better have a shower before I break the news.Let's get ready to face it."

He quickly got done with the shower and took some time to mentally prepare himself.

"I am all set to tell them now. They must have been waiting for it since last night. Let's prepare for the initial shock."

He steps out of his room after taking a deep breath and drinking a couple of glasses of water.He looked for his mom, and as he found her, he said, Mom, I want to tell you something very important.

I know what you want to tell us, and I can't wait to hear it, beta (son), but you better tell us in the evening because both your papa and Sanskriti are not home now as they left very early today, Mamta said.

But mama, I want to tell you now, Amar said hesitantly.

Amar beta(son), I am busy now, and even if you tell me now, later on you have to tell your papa and Sanskriti as well. It's better you tell us in the evening when everyone is home, requested Mamta.

After this, Amar went to his room and decline to eat breakfast as well.

"Things have not started the way I wanted them to, as I couldn't break the news in front of them.I was mentally so ready to tell them, but now I have to wait for hours to do it.By afternoon, I could have felt the initial impact, but now I can't.It is like hanging on the edge of a cliff and not knowing when you are going to fall. My situation can be compared to have slow poison and waiting for death to arrive.I was very confident that I could face the initial impact after breaking the news, but now I am feeling shaky from the inside. The confidence I had about 30 minutes ago has been shattered and transformed into fear."

"There is no turning back now, Amar, as you have already told Mama that you are going to tell them what is troubling you, and I guess you better execute the experiment."

"Yes, I will, but what am I going to do till the time Papa arrives home?"

"I guess you better do something similar what you have been doing for past few days. Instead of wasting time, better use it to learn something. This will calm your mind and make you feel better.

"Yes, I guess that is the right idea."

Amar got busy reading a few articles about his favourite topics, like conspiracy theories and green energy.

Finally, after a while, he started feeling better and really got into reading.

He keeps reading, and the clock has just ticked over 1 p.m.

Mamta called him for lunch, to which he declined and said, I am not feeling well now, and I guess I will only eat after I reveal the truth to all of you.

Mamta understands that he is already anxious about something, so she didn't feel like forcing him further. He stayed in front of his computer all afternoon, and Nischint finally arrived in the evening.Now everyone is home, including Sanskriti.

As soon as Nischint met Mamta, the first thing he asked was, Did he say anything about what is troubling him?

He was ready to tell me in the morning, but since you and Sanskriti were not home, I suggested him to tell all of us in the evening, replied Mamta.

Finally he is ready to tell it after hiding it for so many days, said Nischint with a sigh of relief.

Let's quickly go to his room and ask Bhaiya (brother), said Sanskriti.

He spent the entire day in his room. Better we call him out and listen to him here, then we can have dinner together, Mamta suggested.

Yeah, Sanskriti, your mama is absolutely right, said Nischint.

Let me call Bhaiya (brother) out, and then we could talk to him, nodded Sanskriti.

Sanskriti went to Amar's room and asked him to come out to talk to them, to which Amar said, I would be out in a couple of minutes.

"Finally, Amar, the time has come to break the news. Stay strong and remember the plan. Make it happen as naturally as possible. Brace for the Initial Impact of the News"

Amar appears in front of them in the living room after sipping water and taking a deep breath.

I hope you are fully ready now to tell us, said Nischint with a giggle to lighten the atmosphere.

Bhaiya(brother), take that chair and sit down comfortably, suggested Sanskriti.

Amar is now surrounded by three people, all of whom are waiting for him to open his mouth. Amar has prepared himself for this moment for many days, but now he can feel the fear of it. All that mental preparation he has done vanished in the air. It gives him the vibe of having his neck under a sharp sword.

Finally, he uttered the first few words.

Mom, Dad, and Sanskriti, I have gotten myself into a lot of trouble, and it's killing me on the inside. I want to admit it and get rid of that burden from my heart. Due to this, I am not able to sleep properly, eat well, or have any interest in doing anything in life.

Suddenly, Mamta interrupted him. We all know that you are deeply troubled by it, beta (son), and it is quite evident with how you stay in your room the whole day and eat less. We all understand it. So, I suggest you get to the main point, as we are equally anxious and tensed as you are.

The thing that has been troubling me for many days is that I have lost money in an investment and am not able to recover it, said Amar with a stuttering voice.

You lost what? asked Nischint, as he couldn't understand it clearly.

Bhaiya (brother), please speak it clearly, requested Sanskriti.

I have lost money in an investment, said Amar with a loud, distorted voice as he was feeling lethargic due to skipping breakfast and lunch.

You have lost money in an investment. What investment are you talking about? asked Nischint with surprise and shock.

Mom and Dad, I had invested the money in one of the cryptocurrencies, and it has crashed completely, making me unable to even get some value out of it. I realise I made a huge error, and...

Tears have started falling out of Amar's eyes, and with this, he is unable to speak further.

Beta (son), everything was going great, like you have finished teaching your cousin and are now planning to teach more students. Why did you get into this investment, and that too without even discussing it with us? asked Mamta while wiping away his tears.

It's true that I had started making money, but it was quite little. I understand that I need to contribute to the family's income for future things like house renovation and even medical bills. I got under pressure and decided to invest in crypto to make quick and easy money. I failed at it, and I am totally sorry about it, said Amar, with more tears joining the race from his eyes.

Sanskriti quickly gave him the glass of water, as he was exasperated and about to completely break down.

Beta (son), quick money ideas never work. Hard work is the key to success. Only a few people make quick money, and that too is supported by their luck. If you analyse your life journey, you will find tonnes of examples where your hard work has gotten you over the line, not your luck. I worked hard to build this house, and it wasn't done in a day. Hard work and patience go hand in hand to build something big, explained Nischint to Amar in a very polite and easy way.

Mistakes are part of life, and accepting your mistake is always good. Since you have accepted it, now you could rectify it and avoid repeating it in the future as well, added Mamta to Nischint's statement.

Yes, Bhaiya (brother), Cheer up now. There is no need to feel depressed now as you are still young and have enough time to recover from whatever loss you have made, Sanskriti said with a smile.

Yeah, she is right, Amar. Since you will be teaching in the near future, you will be able to get things back on track, said Mamta while reassuring Amar.

I know you are not feeling well now, Amar, so kindly take some rest now, and there is no need to be so worried about investment and loss. Just forget it. The more we think about loss, the further we waste time, Nischint advised him.

He hasn't eaten anything since morning, so you better have dinner before you rest, Amar, requested Mamta.

I am not feeling great now and have no appetite to eat dinner, replied Amar.

It is because you are overstressed, Bhaiya (brother). If you don't want to have dinner, then at least drink some orange juice, requested Sanskriti.

Yeah, go to your room now, Amar, and don't be stressed anymore. Forget about what has happened and look ahead for new opportunities in life, suggested Nischint.

Sanskriti, take this juice glass to Amar's room, said Mamta while handing her over a glass of juice.

Amar moved to his room without realising something important. He finished off the juice and laid in his bed.

"Did I forget to tell them something?"

"Yes, you forgot to say sorry to them while moving back into your room."

"Not this thing. Oh! I got it now. I totally forgot to tell them that I lost that saving, worth 500k rupees. I think they thought I had lost the money I made through teaching. Should I go out and tell them what is left to be said?"

"You can't do it now, Amar, as they are having dinner now. You have to wait till tomorrow to complete what you were supposed to say."

"Tomorrow, I can't wait until the evening. I need to get up early and tell them before Papa leaves for work."

"And since you missed telling them the whole thing at once, tomorrow you could see a difference in their reaction when they learn that you have lost the entire saving in crypto investment."

"Tomorrow again, I needed to be mentally prepared and brace for the real impact."

After setting an early alarm, Amar went to sleep.

That's how the Day 1 of "The Family Experiment" went, and the action moves to Day 2.

The 3rd of April is here, and he is up early courtesy to the early alarm. He quickly finished off his morning routine, including the shower. Finally, he is ready to drop the big shock on his family. He moved out of his room and saw his father and Sankriti having breakfast. As soon as Mamta saw him, she said, Amar, you are up early today. That is good. Come have breakfast with us.

I am not hungry now, and I am up early to tell you something very important that I missed yesterday, replied Amar.

Don't tell us that you made another investment last night and lost money in that too, said Nischint jokingly.

No, I didn't make any investments last night, but I guess yesterday, while telling you about my loss, I forgot to mention how much I lost, said Amar quietly.

Okay, Amar, I am getting late to get ready for work, so it would be great if you could quickly tell us how much it is, requested Nischint.

Amar, your papa is getting late for work. If it is not that urgent, then we could discuss it in the evening, suggested Mamta.

I lost the entire 500k rupees saving we had in my bank account, Amar rushed through the words.

You lost the entire savings, 500k....Nischint struggled to speak the full sentence.

At this moment Amar could see that his father might collapse so, he stopped speaking.

What have you done? You lost entire Savin....These were the last few words Nischint spoke before he rushed out of the house.

Where are you going, papa? Sanskriti shouted with a shock.

As Mamta could see Nischint out of her sight, she got after him as well while yelling, Nischint, what happened to you, and where are you going?

As Sanskriti saw that both Papa and Mama were out of the house, she followed them quickly, and now only Amar has been left in the house. He wanted to ask her to stay here but held himself back because he didn't expect this to happen and in total shock as well.

"What is going on now? At worst, I thought he would yell at me, criticise me, or even slap me, but this is totally unexpected. I am getting worried about his health now. Papa might get a heart attack or go completely insane"

"Why am I getting so negative? Things will be alright," said Amar while sipping some water.

"Let me call Sanskriti and ask her what is happening, as waiting here is going to make me more anxious."

He dialled Sanskriti's number and could hear her phone ringing in the house. Then he dialled Mamta, followed by his father.

"I believe they all left their phones here in haste, but where would they be now? I thought I would be facing the initial impact of the news, but I think it is heading in a different direction now."

"See, Amar, due to your anxiety and fear, you are even sweating in this cold and chilly weather."

"Yeah" said Amar, while wiping off the sweat.

Just after 15 minutes of this event, Amar's anxiety has started going over the limit. He went out to see if he could see any sign of them, but in vain.

"I should go and seek them, but I can't do it as I have no inkling about where they have gone."

For the next 15 minutes, he kept walking into the house and out, hoping to catch a glimpse of them.

Finally, after 30 minutes, Amar heard his phone ring.

"Who is this calling me now? It looks like a landline telephone number."

Amar answered the call quickly because he was worried.

Bhaiya (brother), it's me, Sanskriti. Quickly come to Times Square, and while getting out of the house, make sure to lock it properly. We are all waiting for you here.

How is papa? asked Amar, but the call got ended as soon as he asked it.

Amar quickly locked the main door before rushing towards Time Square. In his haste, he forgot to change his clothes and failed to change from his home slippers to shoes. As he was getting close to Time Square, he tried to focus his sight to find them.

"Where are they exactly? I can't see them," said Amar, while breathing heavily due to being very rapid while walking.

As he looked around, he noticed that in one corner, Papa is sitting on a bench under a tree with his hands on his head, while his mother is seated next to him, saying something that Amar can't understand because he is still far away.

As he started walking towards them, he couldn't keep his head straight and failed to maintain any eye contact. It's like walking in a direction without looking straight and focusing on the ground. There were hardly 20 metres away, but that walk itself seems like a daunting task. The mixed feelings of fear, worry for his father, and uncertainty of what is going to happen are weighing him down so much that his legs are carrying twice the weight of Amar. Finally, Amar's struggle came to an end when he reached to his parents, but was surprised to find Sanskriti nowhere in sight.

As he was about to ask them , someone tapped his shoulder. As he turned around, it was Sanskriti, and before he could ask her something, she said, he is calling you in.

Who is he? Amar inquired, surprised.

Bank Executive is calling you in to ask for some information, replied Sanskriti while going into the bank. Amar followed her.

As he walked in ,the bank executive informed him that his family has requested his account balance and needed his consent to reveal his account balance to them.

In response, Amar nodded to give permission, and the bank executive quickly told Sanskriti the account balance.

As soon as she heard it, she walked out to tell her parents. Amar held himself back as he feared that as soon as they got to know it, there was a high chance of a ruckus in the public place. Amar finally walked out of the bank and stationed himself at a distance from his parents, who were discussing something with Sanskriti.

"I think now they are going to call me, and there is going to be a big public spectacle here."

In the next couple of minutes, Amar saw something that popped his eyes out.

All of them started walking back to the house without even uttering a single word to Amar, despite the fact that they could see him clearly.

"What is going on now? Things are happening exactly in the opposite way as I predicted."

"I think they are in disbelief and shell-shocked by the news, which is why they are not saying anything."

As they walked out of Amar's sight, he started walking to the house as well. He walked past the park where he used to go. It seems like that park pulled Amar in as he walked into the park without having any reason to go there.

He could see withered leaves and dried flowers on the ground.

"Is my life going to be this bleak soon?"

"I believe you are about to go insane from overthinking. You better catch a breath here and walk to the house soon as their anger bomb could drop on you anytime ."

Amar sat there for a while and then started walking back to the house. As he reached the house, he was expecting that there must be a loud discussion going on there, but to his surprise, there was nothing like that. It was a pin-drop silence as he entered the house. So quiet that

Amar could not only feel but also hear his heart racing. He tried to find Papa and Mama but couldn't find them anywhere in the living room.

"Where have they gone? I am sure they came into the house as the front door was unlocked."

As he paid attention, he could hear Sanskriti speaking something. He gets close to her door to hear that clearly.

“Papa won’t be able to come to work today as he is not well. He will call you later to give you an update on his health.”

"She is in her room and informing Papa’s employer that he won't be coming to work, but where are they?"

"I think I got it. They are in their room."

Amar moved closer to his parent’s room and saw that the door was locked from the inside. The whole house was in pin-drop silence, and Amar failed to have enough courage to walk into their room or call them out.

"I think I'll wait outside in the living room, because they'll be out for lunch in the next 30 minutes."

Amar waited outside for more than 45 minutes, but no one came out of the room.

"It's strange that no one is moving out of the room while it's well past the usual lunch time."

As nobody moved out, Amar moved into his room as he got tired of waiting for them.

"Is it the calmness before the storm really hits me? As of now, things are very unpredictable, and I am worried about Papa’s health as well. Even they skipped lunch as well, and I don't know... Should I tell them the truth and stop this experiment right now as I am getting worried about Papa?"

"Once you get their full reaction, I guess that could be the earliest time to abort it, as you have faced a lot, so just wait for a while. At least face the initial impact of it."

Amar wants this time to pass quickly so he can face them, but at the same time, every passing second is making him worried as well. It's like anger is filling inside them like air does in a balloon, and the longer the air goes, the more it stretches the balloon, with a high chance of a bigger burst. As lunch time is long gone and time is heading for early evening, Amar starts feeling low on energy and hungry as well.

"I think I need to either eat something or take some rest."

He chose the second option, and it didn't take him much time to fall asleep. He woke up to a loud noise of someone knocking on his door and shouting. "Amar, get out now and open the door." Amar was in such a deep sleep that it took him a couple of minutes to figure out whether he was still in a dream or not and who is at the door.

"Oh, it's mama!"

"Yes, I will be out in two minutes," Amar said as the knocking stopped.

"I think the hardest part of this experiment has come, and I better be ready to face it," said Amar before he counted to ten to give him a breather timer.

As he walked, he could feel the storm in the air engulfing him very well. His father was sitting in one corner of the couch, while Mama and Sister were in the other.

Before we say anything, can you say that again to avoid any confusion as Papa is still in disbelief, Sanskriti remarked sarcastically.

I am sorry to…

I think you can keep this sorry drama aside and get straight to the point, said Mamta with strong frustration in her voice.

This is the first arrow shot by Mamta, passing straight through his heart.

Someone who always called him beta(son) and stays by his side in every difficulty is standing in front of him.

I have lost whatever saving we had in that bank account in a crypto investment, said Amar with a loud voice and a flat face without any emotion.

Why not sell this entire house, your mom's jewellery, and even your educational certificate to invest in crypto? Nischint said with a loud groan.

This is the second big arrow Amar has received straight to his heart, and this time it's from his father.

The person who never raised his voice against Amar since he was born is totally frustrated now.

Now you have put my future at jeopardy like you did with yours, retorted Sanskriti.

The final arrow from Sanskriti is out there now.

His lovely young sister, who used to listen to him and always ready to help him out, is totally changed now.

Amar has realised that the way he predicted things was completely wrong. Things have escalated far faster than expected, and it appears that Amar has surrendered, as three people are firing shots at him.

I earned, saved, and protected that saving my entire life, and in the end it was robbed by someone living with us, Nischint yelled at Amar.

This is not what I expected from you, Amar. We thought you had grown up, but your intelligence is even below that of a toddler, added Mamta.

Tell me how I'm going to join the art college. You were the one who showed me my dream and crushed it as well, Sanskriti retorted, venting her rage through words.

"Words cut deeper than a sword" is an apt description of Amar's current situation.

There is no use of telling him anything, as we are all robbed. You better start thinking about some other career options, said Nischint to Sanskriti.

I think we also move to our rooms as there is no hope of positivity left in life, said Mamta with disappointment.

I completely lost my appetite, and I don't want to eat anything now, said Sanskriti to Mamta.

After a brief conversation, all three of them have now entered Sanskriti's room, leaving Amar speechless and completely frozen. As they have moved into the room, there is some discussion going on, which Amar could only hear, though he is not understanding it at all due to the fact that he is completely frozen. He stayed there, like a statue, for almost 10 minutes. This is probably the first time Amar has lost his inner voice for that long. As his lips started getting dry, the sudden urge to drink water brought his senses back to work. He went back into his room to get some water and wash his face in order to feel something because his body was numb. After having water and face washing, he is sitting in bed with tonnes of things to think about.

"Where should I be starting from? There are so many things to think about that even an entire night would be insufficient."

"I think you don't need to feel shocked or even surprised by their behaviour. Firstly, the story you have told them is a big shock for them, and you are also aware of the fact that they were a bit disappointed with you as you were unemployed for so long, and finally that volcano of frustration has erupted with a lot of jolt."

"It was surely more than criticism, as I have been labelled as a robber."

"Don't worry, it is just the frustration and worries they have regarding the future. Surely they were expected to behave like this, and they did. Get out of your Fairy World if you were expecting it to be like yesterday. You should not be worried about how they reacted today as things were quite heated, but be worried about when they calm down and start thinking further as most of the time we skip important things when we are angry."

"Whatever happened today has proven Samridh's words correct about parents."

"Forget about Samridh and his theories. It's not like if he is proven right, he is going to tease you your whole life. He is not even aware of anything going on like this in your life."

"What am I supposed to watch out for now as I can easily term what happened today as initial frustration and anger?"

"As an initial impact, it definitely includes anger and frustration, but the important thing is that when this anger subsides, will they still see lost money only or will they consider you as well? The thing to look out for is whether or not this amount of money has completely taken over your importance, place, or value in the family."

"I think I would end this experiment the moment they put that loss aside for a while and show some signs of care and respect for me. If they don't, then I believe things are going to hit full quota of 10 days."

"One big mistake should never be enough to end someone's career, especially if you are young, and every loss in life has a chance of revival."

"This is probably the first time I skipped whole day of eating."

"Get used to this for at least the next few days."

"Even though I started this experiment, they now have the power to put an end to it. I am just like an object that is going to face everything thrown at him . They can finish it off by tomorrow. We'll see if I make it to 10 days or if they finish it before me. Either my human value , family value, love for me, or my apologies are going to make them realise that their son is in deep trouble and need their support or that money lost is going to keep them totally blind . If everything fails to make them realise it, then surely this thing will make them happy," said Amar while pointing towards the pillow containing money.

After this, Amar laid down while holding the pillow with money and said, "If this experiment goes for the full 10 days, then you win,otherwise, I win if it ends before 10 days. Sorry, we both can't win at the same time."

He went to sleep early after this.

This is the end of day 2 of "The Family Experiment," and action moves to day 3 now.

The 4th of April has arrived, and Amar is awake, but despite an alarm, he has missed it. He saw bright sunlight, which indicates that he is fairly late in getting up. As he tried to get up, he felt quite weak and light.

"Two days into the experiment, it seems like I have lost 1/4th of my weight and no energy at all. I need to find something to eat."

Amar quickly got out of his room after brushing his teeth to find some food. After a few minutes, forget about food, he can't find anyone in the house.

"Where have they gone? Surely they can't still be in rooms.Its sunday today so both Sanskriti and Papa must be home"

Even though Amar is sure that they are not in the house, he still went to check on his parents as well as Sanskriti's room, and as he predicted, both of them were locked from the outside.

"I think they have gone out. Let me call them to find out where they've gone and when they'll be back."

After this, he dialled all of them one by one, but sadly no one picked up the call, and after calling them multiple times, he finally gave up. He shifted his attention from where they were to where the food is. His gaze was drawn to the dinner table, where food was kept.

"I think they kept the food for me, so let's have it first before I focus on other things."

He finished the food quickly as his hunger was very strong and started waiting for them. It is almost afternoon, and there is no sight of them. His patience has started running out, so he went out of the house to have a look, but nothing was there either. Finally, he gets tired of waiting and goes to his room . As soon as he gets in bed, he heard someone entering the house.

"I think they are back, but where were they? Well, let me go out and find out."

As he was about to get out of bed, he suddenly felt back pain.

"I think due to improper body position while sleeping last night, it's causing trouble in my back. They are just back. I'd better wait here for a while, then go out."

He stayed in and paid attention to the discussion going on outside in the living room.

Now how are we going to pay medical bills if your health doesn't improve? Mamta said.

My health is fine. It's just that I get extremely worried about how we are going to afford Sanskriti Education, and this house is also getting old. We need money for her education, house renovation, and her marriage as well, replied Nischint with concern.

Papa, don't be stressed now. Take this medicine and remember that the doctor told you not to stress, Sanskriti advised.

Yeah, she is absolutely right. What has happened can't be changed, but we can try our best not to be stressed about it. Now lets have some rest as we have been mentally stressed since yesterday and physically tired since morning,suggested Mamta.

After this, Amar could hear their feet making noises as they went into their rooms.

"I got it where they went. As Papa was not feeling well, they all went to a doctor and most likely got some medical checkups as well. I am getting worried about Papa. Should I tell them the truth as he is getting stressed about it?"

"I think you should apologise to them, especially Papa, and let's hope that they forgive you and get ready to give you a chance. The moment they forgive you, you can end this experiment, and all the worries will be gone. I know you are worried about them, but it would be great if they showed a bit of care for you as well. As they understand that you are in a lot of trouble as well, and they have said enough strong words to you as well. They all are so angry with you that even if you tell them the truth, they will further vent their anger on you, and you will be in even bigger trouble than what you are in now, Amar. Either they calm down and think about you, restoring your faith in human values being more important than money, or you let this experiment run for 10 days, as after 10 days they will be calmer and it will be easier for you to explain why you chose this experiment."

"Yes, let's see what happens in the evening, as I have already started feeling lonely and even my jaw is locking due to not speaking with anyone for some time."

Finally, evening has arrived, and Amar is planning to apologise, hoping that they will show some concern for him and he will be able to quickly exit this experiment that is leaving him extremely alone. He walked out and saw all of them sitting on couch and watching television. At first glance, he could see his father physically well , which is a good sign for his health.

I would like to talk about something important to you all, said Amar politely.

As soon as they heard it, Nischint asked Sanskriti to turn off the television.

"I think this is a good opportunity for me to convince them, and maybe if I am lucky enough, this thing could end by today or tomorrow itself ", Amar thought in mind.

Yes, What you want to say, say now, said Mamta still full of anger.

Amar realised that anger is still there, and his desires to see this experiment ending soon are very slim.

I want to firstly say that I am extremely sorry for what has happened. I take full responsibility of money loss, and I am not running away from it. I understand that money was kept for Sanskriti's education. It could have been used for anything, including house renovation. By the time Amar finished these lines, his voice has started vanishing behind tears. He took a pause, wiped his tears, and took a deep breath.

As you know, I will be finding more students to teach. I will start making money soon , and I am sure I will be able to save enough to afford Sanskriti's education. I am really sorry again, and I am... Amar's throat started getting dried and his voice got distorted.

The stunt you have done to bankrupt us is not a mistake but a crime. Any trust we had in you is now completely gone, Nischint responded with loud yelling.

We did whatever you said. You chose to have engineering, and we spent money. You chose not to join any job after studying, and we were fine with that. We gave you food, clothes, and respect. What did you give us in the end? This is the love, care, and respect you have for us. Forget about us. You didn't even think about Sanskriti and her future, Mamta added more fuel to the fire faced by Amar.

I didn't do it intentionally. I want to make money for all of us. I invested with the hope that I would make enough to not only afford Sanskriti's education but also renovate this house, use it on Sanskriti's marriage, and have some in the form of saving so that you could retire early as well, papa, said Amar loudly in anger and frustration.

Then suddenly he realised that speaking in anger wouldn't work here, and he quickly toned his voice down.

I accept that it was my mistake, a big one, and I am fully aware that it's a big amount, but I deserve a chance to rectify it. I accept that I lost money, but I had no intention of getting you into trouble. I just wanted to make things better for all of us, and things didn't go according to the plan, said Amar in a very polite and calm way.

Say thank you to God that you got a chance to stay in the house, have food, and still have clothes on your body.We are all kind enough to keep you in this house rather than throwing you out and leaving you homeless, foodless, and clothless, Nischint said with the same rage Amar displayed a few minutes before.

We would have done exactly what Papa has said, but we backed out due to society's and relative's pressure. We don't want to face the common question of society that "Why did you throw Amar out?" Then we'd have to tell them the whole story and become the laughingstock of the entire world. At your age, people are buying houses, cars, and other precious things for their families, whereas you have certainly made us appear as idiots , added Mamta to what Nischint said.

My friends and teachers had been asking me about which art college will I be joining for the past couple of weeks. What am I going to tell them when I go to school? I can't tell them that my brother has lost the money kept for my education, so I can't be joining the art college now, said Sanskriti in a sarcastic tone.

Same here. Even when my boss asked what had happened to my health suddenly, I had to lie that it was due to change in the weather, Nischint added further.

I am having headache now due to this daily yelling , frustration, and overthinking, Nischint said to Mamta.

Papa, you should rest now because you'll be back to work tomorrow, Sanskriti gave a piece of advice.

Kindly make us two cups of tea , said Mamta as they moved into the room and Sanskriti went to the kitchen to make tea.

Amar was left alone in the living room now.

"As I can see their anger is getting higher day by day and things are going from bad to worst, I think I should go to the kitchen to talk to Sanskriti to get some idea of what is going on in her mind."

Once this thought came into his mind, he quickly made his way to the kitchen.

As he reached her, she was busy making tea.

Listen, Sanskriti, trust me that I would be able to earn enough to get you into art college, and I want you to make them understand that it is my first financial mistake, and one mistake can't finish off my career.

Give me two minutes, as I need to give them tea, said Sanskriti.

As she went to give them Tea , Amar saw an opportunity to end this experiment through her.

“I think if I am able to convince her, then surely she can try to convince them as well. They are angry with me, but surely she can make them understand very well. Maybe if she tries, they will understand that since money is lost, at least they should try to support me in this situation.”

As Amar was going through his thoughts, he could see her coming back.

I can try once to consider what you have said about earning and all, but I don't think they are going to forgive you , going by the current anger and frustration they are having.You have not only broken their trust but broken them completely as well, said Sanskriti before going to her room.

Amar is again left alone in the kitchen, and it's late in the evening, so he didn't spend much time there and moved into his room as well.

As he returned to his room, he was exhausted from the stress and constant thrashing he was experiencing. He laid down in his bed and started thinking.

"Papa and Mama are acting very extreme. Either this house is extremely quiet and I am feeling lonely, or we are having loud arguments full of anger and frustration."

"I think this experiment is taking shapes and forms with every passing day."

"What do you mean by taking different forms?" Amar coughed loudly.

"I think you are having a cough due to the change in weather. In different forms or shapes, as on the first day, they were so nice and didn't say much to you, as they thought you had lost only what you had earned. The second day was the real impact day, and you lost control of the experiment as things went too far. The second day created two possible outcomes: either money wins or your human value and respect win. You had hoped that by the third day, things would have calmed down and the experiment would be over, but that didn't happen. Your emotional appeal and polite behaviour failed to take over the money power."

"So what do you think day four is going to bring?"

"I think now it's becoming more of an ego battle. They are keeping their noses high and thinking about the money being lost. Even your attempt to convince them that you would earn it back has failed terribly. They are totally adamant that you don't deserve a chance to get back your human value and respect in the family, even if you try to assure them that you can rectify your mistake."

"And how about the other ego?"

"The other ego is yours, Amar. You can see them that they are angry ,frustrated, and are not concerned about their son. They might be forgetting their parental duties to understand that it is entirely possible for you to get back what is being lost, and they can show a bit of trust as well. At the same time, you are adamant about continuing the experiment, and you want to see how long they will continue to think about money by criticising and ignoring your importance in their lives."

"I understand their suffering and am ready to end this experiment, as I can't see them in trouble as well, but at least they get ready to give me a chance in life. I am being called a robber and someone who made them bankrupt. They are ready to throw me out of the house and let me suffer."

"Here you go again. As I just said, this battle of ego will take this experiment 10 full days, and ultimately, it seems like money will win because you can't take this trashing forever and expect them to realise your value. They only have 7 days left, or possibly less if you give up due to the extreme physical and mental stress you are experiencing."

"I may be under extreme stress, but I believe I can last for 10 days and see this experiment ending as well. I think tomorrow there is a chance that things might be easy as Papa will be going to his job and Sanskriti will go to her school as well. Mama would be alone, and she might think about me as well, which could lead to some sort of truce between them and I. Things might change, and the experiment might end if they calm down a little."

"Yeah, it's a moving day for sure, and I expect things to get better as well."

"I think that's all I have for today, and I'm going to bed early because there is no energy left in my body . Perhaps the tide will turn tomorrow."

Amar checked his alarm, which was set for early in the morning, and tried to sleep.

That concludes Day 3 of "The Family Experiment," as we move on to Day 4.

Good morning, April 5th. Is this going to be a really good morning for Amar or not? We'll figure it out in a while as Amar's alarm is about to go off.

Finally, the alarm goes off, and he is up. As he tried to get up now, he could feel that his body was not responding very well.

"I think I need to fix my eating, otherwise, I might collapse soon. Let me check my weight."

As Amar weighed himself, he was shocked to see the result.

"I measured it on 1st April , and now it's 5th April . I've lost 3 kilograms. This stress might not seem very hard on me mentally, as I have had some amount of it always present in my mind, but my body is certainly giving up. I need to eat whatever I get and whenever I get it to stop the weight loss."

He quickly brushed his teeth, followed by a shower. After the shower, he realised that his hair fall rate has become rapid.

"It appears that with weight, even the hair are falling down. Previously, I experienced minor hair loss, but now I am experiencing large amounts of it. I better try not to get too stressed, even if things get harsh, as even if everything fails to convince them by the end of 10 days, I could simply show them the money and sincerely apologise again."

"But first, before you collapse on the fourth day of the experiment, go out and eat something."

As he went out, he saw Papa and Sanskriti eating. He doesn't feel like going there and joining them, as they could get angry again and leave the breakfast, so he came back to his room.

"It's good to see that Papa is eating now with Sanskriti. Soon he would leave with Sanskriti for his work while she would go to her school. Finally, I could see things getting back on track as they used to be before this experiment," said Amar with a smile.

When he saw them happy, he forgot about his pain and stress. A half hour later, Amar went out. He noticed that both the dine-in room and the living room were empty. He looked around to find his mom, but she was not there.

"Where could she have gone? I know Papa and Sanskriti are going to work and school, respectively, but where is she?"

As he was going through it, he suddenly saw food being kept on the dinner table.

"I think that is kept for me, as they don't want to ask me to join them while eating or tell me that they kept it on the table. I better have it first before making any move."

He quickly finished it off and even washed dishes in the kitchen so that Mama would have some ease. After a while, he saw his mom entering the house. She is carrying a lot of vegetables and some household items. This is probably the first time in many many years she has bought all these things, as it is always done by Amar.

"These are certainly ominous signs for the situation getting any better, but let me try to see what the current status is."

Let me help you put these vegetables in the refrigerator, mama, said Amar in an extremely polite and calm way.

I will manage it. You don't need to be worried about us, said Mamta while going away towards the kitchen.

This severely harmed Amar's confidence in making any kind of small talk with her. He waited almost half an hour there, looking at her like a thirsty looks at a river, and she completely ignored him while doing her work.

"I believe my luck has run out of steam now, and it appears that I should go back to my room as there is no hope of me making small talk with her."

He moved to his room and, to pass time, started reading articles on his computer. He couldn't concentrate even just after five minutes of reading because his mind was racing back and forth, wondering what would happen next.

"I will try again in the evening when papa is home from work to convince them that I deserve a chance. As he is now at work, this may help to break his mind's connection to this situation, and then my humble request may melt their hearts, and they will finally be ready to accept me as I was before this experiment."

"Yeah, and since you are not getting enough food to eat, you better save energy for the evening."

"Yeah, as I am already feeling low energy, and my blood pressure might be falling as well."

"Yeah, as tomorrow could be quite similar to today and there would be nothing to do for you after 10 a.m., then you better go to the doctor and get your blood pressure checked."

"Yeah true. That way I could spend some time outside while getting my health checked as well."

After this, Amar went to sleep with the intention of passing most of the time while sleeping before Papa arrives from work. Finally, evening is here. Nischint has just arrived from work, and Amar is up also.

"I think I'd better wait for a while before going out and trying to convince them. Let Papa have some tea and relax because I'm sure things will be stressful for him while I'm talking to them."

Amar waited for about an hour, and during this time he could hear that Papa has finished his tea and some conversation about how his work went and all that.

Finally, Amar decided to go out and try to convince them.

He goes out and says with the utmost politeness, I know you are still angry at me and have been ignoring me, but I want to tell you that leaving me alone is torturing me mentally. My energy levels are low, my blood pressure is dropping, and my hair is falling out at an alarming rate. If you continue like this, I may be surrounded by more stress and anxiety. I accept my mistake, and I should be given a chance for repentance.

Now you want us to be nice and kind with you as your health is not okay while you have distorted our future, health, and mental peace for ever , Nischint was still fuming with anger.

Whatever health issues you are having are created by you alone. You never got any job after finishing off your studies and began spending your days in your room. Since you've finished two months of teaching, you spend the entire day in your room. Go out, walk, and even go running to fix it, said Mamta with frustration.

We don't have money to fix our health since you made us bankrupt, How are we going to afford your medical tests? Tell me, Nischint asked to Amar, with frustration.

I am not asking for any medical attention. I only need your emotional support. I can start going for a jog and even start running to fix my health issue. What I am seeking is that you give me a chance and show a bit of trust on me, and I will be able to earn the major part of the loss within one year, requested Amar politely.

We have trusted you once, and that has proven to be our biggest mistake. We gave you all of our saving to save in your bank account, and ultimately you embezzled it all. We don't want to lose our house and even our future saving to you, so there is no chance we are going to trust you, said Nischint while coughing.

As Mamta saw him coughing, she immediately said to Amar, There's no need to bother us by saying the same thing over and over. Your constant approach to the same issue is making Nischint uneasy. How are we going to even buy food if he gets sick again? There is no one who could feed us, including you.

As soon as she said it, it hits Amar hard. He quickly moved out of there to his room. He sat down for a while and tried to gather his thoughts.

"I think there is no hope today, that this is going to get any better."

It was 07:45 p.m. when Amar looked at the clock.

"Since there is no hope left for today, I better use this time for something else."

"I suggest you better go out for a walk as it would help you to disconnect your mind from this stressed environment for a while and it would be good for your health as well."

He puts on his shoes, gloves, winter cap , and went for a walk. He walked slowly as he realised that, due to cold, not many people were out. His body gave up walking quickly, and his breathing rate increased.

"I think I need to sit down before I move more."

Then he realised that the park was just a few steps away. He went there and felt that it has been so many days since his last visit, though the truth is that only a few days ago he was there. He sat down on the bench he used to sit.

"Look at these dried leaves that are under my feet. My life is going like this exactly. I am crushed under everything. My value, respect, and position have fallen the same way these leaves have fallen from the tree."

Then he looked up at the tree he was sitting beneath.

"Sadly, these leaves can't grow up again on the tree, but surely, in a week, I will be shining and fresh like those new leaves on the tree."

"Don't forget that you have to meet Samridh after this experiment wraps up."

"Yeah, I always have that thing in my mind."

Amar spent the next 30 minutes looking here and there.

"It's dark and foggy now, and I should start moving towards the house. I may not get dinner again and need to sleep without it."

He began his slow journey towards the house, and after a bit of exhaustion, he arrived.

They were eating when he arrived. He walked straight to his room rather than joining them. As usual, nobody asked him to join as well.

"I better catch my breath before moving out to eat dinner."

He had some water followed by a quick face wiping session. As he moved out, he was shocked to see that nobody was there.

"It has hardly been 10 minutes since I got home, and they all are done with food and in rooms now. What a time I am having ! When I was in college, I used to get home sometimes around 10 p.m., and they all used to wait and eat with me, and now they can't even stay for 10 minutes since I got home."

After that, he saw food being kept on the dinner table.

"I think that is my dinner. I better have it quickly, as there is no sense in spending much time outside here."

While eating, he realised food is indeed delicious, but what he is going through has killed his appetite a lot. He ate it quickly and then washed the dish in which he had eaten it. He is in bed now and feeling something very strange.

"They are cooking food for me and washing my clothes. Isn't it a kind of care, though indirectly they are showing for me, but they are still very angry in person?"

"Yes, it could be termed "care," but that is an indirect suggestion that we are keeping you alive. If they want to show care, want to forgive you, or want to give you a chance, they would say it straight. Ask yourself, Even if they kept food for you or washed your clothes daily, would you feel inspired to do anything in life? Will this kind of support help you feel your family's touch, emotions, or care?"

"I think you are right. I thought that their anger was going to last for a couple of days, but it has not. I understand that my error was significant, but I am confident that in two years' time, I would be able to recoup the money had I lost it in real. In reality, if they show a bit of care and respect, their money gets doubled, as I still have that money, plus the care and respect shown by them would encourage me to earn the same amount of money in two years. If you are supported by people around you, you can overcome any problem in life, and if you are left stranded with no human touch, you would find it hard to even breathe."

"Calm down, Amar. There is no use of getting angry here as it's not good for your health."

"Oh, I remember that tomorrow, after so-called breakfast, I need to go for my medical test as well. Luckily, I have some money left from two months of teaching that should cover at least a blood pressure test."

"Yeah, you better care for your health as well as it's going down at a rapid rate."

"I totally forgot one thing. As I went out to the park, did they try to search my room?"

Amar looked around to see if anything was out of place, and surprising enough, everything was at its proper place.

"I think no one came to my room. Even my pillow is exactly at the same place as it was. It seems like they are fully convinced that I have lost the money, and they didn't even care to search for them in my room."

(After a small pause)

"I think it's time for me to go to bed, and we'll see what happens tomorrow. My hopes are vanishing as tomorrow I would be at the halfway mark of the experiment, and the past experiences are strongly suggesting that it is going to go to the full 10 days."

"Yeah, it seems like it, and you better not plan anything now as things are not going according to plan. Just go with the flow and try to seize any opportunity if you get to convince them."

"Yeah, that's the right approach, I believe. Things got a little bit better today in terms of Papa going to work and Sanskriti going to school as well . One key thing I noticed is that they are trying to become completely independent now, as Mama went to buy groceries and other household things."

"It appears that they are completely separating you from the family, and I hope that things don't get too far so that even after you tell them the truth, they keep you at bay."

"That's the new worry I'm having today, and I'm hoping things don't fall apart too badly."

"Yeah, let's go to sleep now because you have to go for a medical test tomorrow."

As Amar finally went to sleep, that marked the 4th day of "The Family Experiment," and finally, we are about to enter the day that will mark the halfway point.

Halfway is here!

Hello and good morning, April 6th! We all know what Amar does early in the morning. We are all used to it now, and it seems like Amar is getting used to this new world where he is completely isolated. With barely 25 words, he is speaking with family members, and most of the time he is just quiet. He waited for Papa and Sanskriti to finish breakfast and leave the house. He went out and saw the food lying on the dinner table. He finished it quickly and got ready to leave the house for medical tests. As he was about to leave the house, Mamta saw him going out.

"I am sure Mama is going to ask me now where I am going and when I will be back."

He kept staring at her for a few minutes, hoping she would say exactly what he predicted, but alas! Nothing like that happened.

Tears were on the verge of falling out of his eyes, but he didn't want to show them to her, so he quickly exited the house. As he was moving towards the medical clinic, he went into deep thoughts.

"This is the first time that I left the house without telling her, and she also didn't ask me for the first time where I was going. These too many first-time things are getting hard to handle," said Amar while wiping off his tears, which were almost touching his jawline.

He is walking with his body only, as his mind is totally somewhere else. Suddenly, his focus went back to the road when he realised that he has reached the medical clinic.

He went for a blood pressure check, followed by an instant blood sugar test. As he expected , both blood pressure and sugar level were down. The doctor said that due to extreme stress and anxiety, blood pressure is dropping, and less eating is making blood sugar drop. Rapid hair fall is also the fruit of what he is going through. The doctor suggested he reduces anxiety, eat well, get proper sleep, and do more physical activities.

Once he gets done with the doctor, he starts moving towards his house.

"Today I am going to take a break from begging in front of them and give my mind and body some rest. This way, they would also get some respite from my requests and issues. It will also show them that I have a bit of self-respect and confidence in myself."

"Since you know the usual pattern very well now, food would be on the dinner table as you arrive home.You eat it, followed by some rest, go for a walk, and then come back to have dinner."

"I always wanted to get my life settled, and now that it has become so predictable, I am not enjoying it at all."

"Yeah, and after 5 days when you tell them the truth, hopefully things will be back to normal, and you will again be complaining about life being very unpredictable."

"Life is always going to be tough, and only I can get strong and face it."

"Well, enough philosophy now, Amar, as you have reached home and Its time to come back to reality."

As he entered the house, he saw something and said, "You are the modern Nostradamus. What a prediction! The food is there at the table!"

He did what he had in his mind , which included eating followed by rest. Papa and Sankriti are both home now. Amar has also awoken from his sleep.

"If they are hoping that I will be requesting or begging, then sorry, mummy and papa, I am going to disappoint you today ."

He quickly put on more clothes and got ready to get out. As he came out of his room, it seemed like all of them got alert and stopped talking to each other. The whole moment can be described as if they have suddenly seen a lion and it made them frozen in total silence. They were fully prepared to counter any argument made by him, but Amar walked straight pass by them and got out of the house.

"I think getting past by them without talking is the hardest part for me, but I am left with no option. I don't want to put them under too much pressure, and I need to see my own health as well"

"Amar, since you're out, you shouldn't keep thinking about that thing. Better start jogging to get your health better."

Amar started jogging at a brisk pace. After doing it for 15 minutes, he rested for a while and started the second round.

"Today I am feeling much better than yesterday, as I have both morning and afternoon meal. I think I am done with physical exercise, and it's time to go back to the house now."

"I suggest you better spend some more time here, as there is nothing there for you to do. Go to the house late enough that by the time you arrive, they would have finished dinner, and you would be able to eat it in peace as well."

"Yeah, I better go to the park and sit there in peace to get some relaxation, both physically and mentally."

He went to the park and sat down on his favourite bench.

While sitting there, he admired the trees and newly bloomed flowers. Cold chilly wind is giving him the vibe of mountains.

"It seems like this park is my new best friend. It always welcomes me whenever I come here with fresh air, fragrance, immense positivity, and a lot of greenery."

As he is looking at the sky, he realises that the moon is out now and that it is time to proceed to the house. He entered the house and was surprised to see that it was dark there. It gives off the vibes of a cemetery, with silence all around and darkness prevailing.

"I believe they slept because I arrived home late.Well, now I am used to these things. Let's have a quick dinner before I reflect on the day."

While eating dinner, suddenly his memory flashed back to school life, and he remembered uncle Pardeep, who used to be a peon at his school.

"Now I can understand his condition as someone who was living here alone while his family was living far from him in..."

"I think you should finish off dinner then discuss all this, as while discussing, your food is getting extremely cold, which was cold already when you started eating it."

Amar quickly finished the remaining food before he could continue Uncle Pardeep's flashback. He is in bed now and has started thinking about his flashback regarding Uncle Pardeep.

"Today I understand why he used to be so happy whenever we had summer holidays and he used to go to his village and stay with his family for one and a half months. I don't even have an idea where he would be now, but back then he was staying here in a small rented room alone, working in school from morning to afternoon, then eating alone, cooking alone, and sleeping alone as well. He did it for so many years. Today, when I don't talk to people around me and eat alone, I can totally understand what we went through, but he was strong enough to get through that time. He went through it over years, not days or months. Despite all this, I never saw him sad or complaining about anything. Enjoying his work every day and always being on time"

"It seems like facing extreme stress and pain has given you the power to understand people's pain and what they went through."

"Yeah, being in a situation quite similar to Pardeep uncle's situation is finally helping me understand how strong he was mentally and emotionally. He must have been under work stress, and then he was staying alone the whole time, but his courage and ability to never give up helped him thrive in life."

"Yeah, and I think once you get done with this experiment and staycation, you try to find Uncle Pardeep and see how he is doing in life. Surely he has inspired you to stay strong even when the situation is totally terrible."

"Yeah, and not only find him but also thank him for changing my perspective about life and loneliness."

"Absolutely correct, and how do you see this experiment shaping up?"

"I think the whole experiment has shaped itself. The same kind of things are going to continue for the rest of the experiment. I will be eating alone. They would be ignoring and avoiding me, and I am going to face some extreme stress and anxiety for the next 5 days."

"And how about you try to convince them?"

"I think I can only convince them if they talk to me properly. If they keep ignoring me or talking to me in anger, then how could I do that?"

"Yeah, that is absolutely right. So are you going to keep requesting them for the next 5 days?

"I believe requesting them will irritate both them and I, so I should do some actions."

"What action are you talking about, Amar?"

"As you know very well, actions speak louder than words, so I am going to start doing some simple household work to make them realise that I still have some value and I am not worthless, rather than requesting them."

"It means you are going to change the whole strategy."

"Yeah, I guess so."

"So what small things do you think you could do in the house?"

"Well, a few of them I have in mind are washing my own clothes, mopping the whole house, and maybe one or two more."

"Well, best of luck with them tomorrow, and I am not 100% sure that they are going to be impressed with it, but surely doing these physical activities would help you get your health better."

"It's the equivalent of killing two birds with one stone, isn't it?"

"Well, you may try because one bird would surely be down but the other one is doubtful, but maybe when you tell them the truth after the completion of the experiment, they will surely appreciate it as well. It's time to sleep now for you as it could be a big day tomorrow with some twists and turns."

"Yeah, surely. Let me look at the money, and rest assured that if my small household works failed to increase my worth in life, that money will."

Amar is ready to sleep in some kind of peace, as he is halfway done with the experiment and very eager to show his strong working actions from tomorrow on. This concludes a strong yet very simple 5th day of "The Family Experiment," and we proceed to day number 6.

Ladies and gentlemen, please greet the 7th of April, an unexpected morning. A good surprise or a bad one? Wait a minute as Amar is up, not because of the alarm but due to the loud noises that are shaking the entire house.

"Why are they so loud early in the morning?"

As he paid attention to what was being discussed outside.

It's early in the morning, and we're in trouble. Now if this water geyser doesn't get repaired soon, how am I going to shower in this cold weather? Amar heard Mamta saying it.

You could choose to shower a bit later in the day, but I can't, as I have to shower early in the morning to go to work. If I shower with cold water, I get shivering all day long at work, Nischint responded.

I have put some water on the gas burner to heat up. Use that water to wash your face, at least for now, and later take a shower once this water geyser is fixed, suggested Mamta.

How am I going to go to school? said Sanskriti.

Once Papa's water is hot, take it off and put some in for yourself as well, said Mamta to Sanskriti.

After listening to the conversation, Amar understood the whole situation.

"The water geyser is broken, and that's why this spectacle is going on. Let me go out and have a look at it and call the electrician to get it fixed quickly."

As soon as he got out and walked towards the bathroom, he was interrupted by Nischint.

No need to have a look at it. You better keep yourself out of house matters. It's all happening because of you, said Nischint while putting Amar away by holding his arm.

I'm just wondering what happened to it and how I'm responsible for this broken water geyser, Amar says frustratedly.

You are the only one responsible for the fact that we have no hot water to shower today. Had you not burned our hard-earned saving, we would have bought a new one, Mamta replied sarcastically.

"They have totally gone mad and blaming me for anything happening in the house," said Amar to himself without being heard.

Let me call the electrician and get it fixed, Amar offered assistance.

As I said a while back , you don't need to get involved in anything. Just enjoy free food, shelter, clothes, and spare us from your curse, said Nischint while folding his hands and bowing in front of him.

This thing hit Amar hardly and he left the place and got back into his room while shaking his head.

"I planned to create a good impression in their eyes today, but they have different ideas in their minds. Now I don't feel like doing any work at all. They seem crazy now and I am getting blamed for things I have no role in."

"Whenever they are in trouble, they would remember that loss and would blame you."

"There is another thing, whenever they get into money trouble and they see me, they start fuming with anger."

"So it seems like earlier they were avoiding you, and now you need to avoid them."

"I don't know anything now. I need some peace now."

As Amar settled down to enjoy some peace, he could hear noises outside.

This guy has been giving us trouble since childhood, but we were young and somehow managed it. Now that we are old and still having a lot of problems because of him, Nischint said to Mamta.

Now how are we going to afford the amount needed to get this geyser fixed, and if it is beyond repair, how are we going to afford a new one? asked Mamta.

Mama, I remember now that I need 2,000 rupees on this coming Sunday as i am going on a school trip to a book fair, informed Sanskriti.

As you can see, all money issues are converging. Either this water geyser can be fixed or she can have 2,000 , you decide, Nischint, as my money management can't face this financial crisis, responded Mamta.

I suggest... Nischint's voice started fading as Amar put earpieces in his ears with full music blast.

"I can't take this much mental torture. I better avoid listening to their sharp words, which are cutting me into many pieces and i am loosing my sanity as well."

He kept the music on, took a notebook, and started writing down things he wanted to do in next 6 months.

"At least in the next 6 months, I should be financially independent. My tuition classes should be good enough that I could afford my expenditure and have some saving as well."

"Yes, the time has come for you to become financially independent. Who knows that even once this experiment is over, they will still blame you for everything, so in that case, getting financial independence would be a great panacea for you"

"Absolutely correct"

"It seems like they are not noisy outside."

Amar cut the music, tried to listen, and it was quiet there.

"It seems like the storm has settled now. Finally, some relief for my ears and mind."

As Amar walked out of the room, he was surprised to see that no one was there.

"I think they have taken the water geyser with them to get it fixed. Let me enjoy this peace in the house before they get back and slaughter me again."

"Oh, food is there, and I am getting so used to it."

He enjoyed sitting on the couch, looking at the clock in the living room, and even watched Television.

"Hashhh! After so long, I enjoyed these things that I used to do during college days."

Suddenly, he heard them outside the house.

"I think they have come back, and I better get away from here to avoid anymore bashing for now."

Amar ran into his room as quickly as a deer would run the moment he saw a tiger or a lion. He could hear them entering the house.

"I didn't hear anything that happened outside earlier because I was listening to loud music. As I can hear Papa and Sanskriti talking outside, it means they didn't go to work and school, respectively."

Luckily, it didn't cost us a lot to get this water geyser fixed, said Mamta.

More importantly, it was fixed quickly, so there would be no problem, at least with hot water, from tomorrow, Nischint responded.

"Fortunately, it's fixed now, and they'll stop blaming me as well,"said Amar while listening to them carefully .

What time are we going to bank to open a new bank account for Sanskriti? Mamta asked.

The bank executive told us to be there after lunch, which ends by 3 p.m., responded Nischint.

See, Sanskriti, he has broken our trust, so whatever work he was managing needed to be done by you. We are going to open a bank account for you today. Now you have to take responsibility of paying electricity bills, water bills and even buying groceries. Whatever saving we are going to have, you need to get them deposited in the bank account. One has made us bankrupt, at least now you step up and take these responsibilities, said Mamta.

"Their preparation is a clear indication that they are moving over me at a rapid pace. They want to give every single work i was doing in family to Sanskriti now."

Amar could feel his heart getting heavier as he is unable to accept these changes.

"I can't even cry as I don't know how long I will be crying. Even my tears are dried now. One mistake, and I am finished for this family. My endless contributions, made through so many small works, were done and dusted in the matter of 5 days only. Now I am on the verge of being completely overlooked, and they want to completely cut me off from this family. I just……"

Amar started breathing heavily and felt some discomfort on his left side of the chest.

"I hope it's not a heart attack as I have so many outstanding things in life." Amar wiped his tears away with his T-shirt.

"Relax Amar. don't worry. It's just that you are hearing a lot of sharp words from them, and it is causing your heart to feel too much pain, and maybe because of that you are having some discomfort."

"Yeah, that sounds true as well. I better take some rest now and get up in the evening to go for my walk."

He puts small cotton buds in his ears to protect himself from their loud noises and sharp words, as listening to loud music causes discomfort in his ears.

He slept, and slept so well that he was totally unconscious for a few hours. He would have continued to sleep if the thunderclap hadn't woken him up. He got up with a sudden surprise and is still in shock.

"Is it already night or evening?"

Amar checked out of the window, and it was raining heavily with a loud thundering sound. He got out of his room and saw most windows being opened and a strong gust of wind getting into the house with droplets of water. He quickly shut all the windows and realised they are still not home.

"I think due to heavy rain they must have stopped somewhere and gotten late to get home. Now I need to wait for the rain to stop, as then only they will arrive. I'll go for my evening walk as soon as they arrive because I don't want to face them and take their hard shots on my heart and mind."

"You better put on those gloves, cap,shocks, and be ready to go out as soon as they come in."

He puts on everything needed to protect himself from the outside cold and even took an umbrella as well.

"How long am I going to wait now as it's getting late ?"

"They should be here anytime soon as the rain has stopped."

"That's what I wanted. Finally, it has stopped."

Amar suddenly heard their footsteps outside the house. He didn't want to face them, so he hid himself in his room. As they entered the house, he could hear them talking about getting drenched in the rain despite taking shelter.

I am going to shower now as I didn't shower in the morning, said Nischint.

Take this new bank account book , debit card and keep them safe in your room, said Mamta to Sanskriti.

Amar noticed a small window to get out of the house without being noticed now as Papa is in the shower, Mama is in the kitchen, and Sanskriti is in her room. He scooted out of his room and got out of the house as well.

"Damn, in my hurry, I forgot to carry that umbrella, and the slight drizzle is still going on."

"It's not that heavy, and if you are too worried about that, go and get the umbrella."

"Leave it. It's better to get drenched rather than face them now. If I go and someone catches me there, my whole mood would take a deep plunge into anxiety again."

Amar started jogging and could hear thunderclap , though the rain was not heavy.

"Today I only had a late breakfast, and I could feel that," said Amar while catching his breath.

"Instead of running for a few minutes followed by a big rest in the park, I better keep walking and feel better."

Now he is walking and thinking about how things are going.

"Though I feel hurt that now they are taking every little task from me and trying to do it by themselves, I think this is how they will realise my value in life."

"They may not realise it if they return all of those small tasks to you after learning the truth, but if they decide not to return all of them to you, then surely they will realise that it was not easy to manage all of them."

"It could be a blessing in disguise for me as well, as if I don't do those little things, I could focus more on my things and have less distractions."

After a while,

"This rain is distracting me a lot, and it's getting heavier as well."

"Take shelter under this tree."

Amar took shelter under a tree, but despite waiting for half an hour, the rain didn't stop.

"I think I need to rush to the house."

Amar rushed to the house but got heavily drenched as he reached .

He quickly got rid of those wet clothes and finished his dinner in complete peace, as no one was there to even say a single word to him.

After dinner, he realised that since he has lost weight and feeling weak, it was easier for common diseases to take over him.

"Since I became weak in just a few days of this experiment, I got cold and cough so easily today with just a few minutes of strong rain."

"Yeah, and since you are feeling extremely cold, that's a sign of fever as well."

"I planned to do so many small tasks today with great zeal but ending it now with misery and fever."(coughing heavily)

"The whole plan to indulge more with them gets washed away with the water geyser breaking down, and finally you are in the bed."

"I am sure tomorrow no one will even ask how am i , though they can hear me coughing heavily in the morning. I have lost all my faith in them as someone who would give me a chance to fix my mistake, and if things keep on going like this, then trust me, even after knowing the truth, the chances of things becoming back to normal are getting slimmer and slimmer."

"Once thing which has happened that ...coughing heavily.....The curtain that was there before this experiment is over now."

"Which curtain are you talking about?"

"Remember earlier also they had concern with you but they never discussed about them in front of you. They discussed it behind your back, but since you told them about this loss, everything has become open."

"Yeah not only open but money loss has added huge amount of fuel into that as well"

" Yes true . Where do you see this experiment heading now?"

"I think I have given up from my side, as all my hopes are dying now . What I predicted today and how it went have nothing in common ."

"It's like a survival thing for you now rather than making some impact."

"Even God wants me to just survive these few days, as I could feel the fever now. If this fever lasts for a few days, by the time I get capable of doing anything, 10 days would be over."

"So it means that what is left to be seen is what happens after 10 days."

"Yeah, since I see no hope of them giving me any respite, let's see what happens when they know the truth."

"Telling them the truth and explaining to them why you took this step is going to be a daunting task for you, Amar."

"Yeah, it could be daunting, but surely not as hard as what I am going through now."

"What if they further get angry and never get back to how they were before the experiment?"

"Well even if it happens, I think I can survive as these 10 days are like training for me on how to stay alone, eat alone, go out alone, and live in total isolation. Coughing heavily……… Even if they don't talk to me much or act in this way, I can manage now as I feel I need to step up in life and get out of my comfort zone."

"Well, let's see how you survive tomorrow. Be prepared to take some more pounding as it's getting intense day by day."

"Yeah, I am fully aware of that, but I strongly believe that I can survive this, as today is the 6th day and 60% of the days are over. I have understood that the less I get in front of them, the better I feel. I better go to sleep now as my fever is getting high now. Let's hope I make it through tomorrow because things are getting tough for me....Coughing loudly while touching his head as it heated up."

Finally, Amar survived the 6th day of "The Family Experiment," and we are all set to witness the 7th day.

On April 8, Amar and them started with a bad morning. Amar is having a high fever, and despite being awake from sleep, he doesn't have the energy to get out of bed. Why is this morning bad for them? Because yesterday's first rain of the winters has done enough to let the water leak through the roof in the form of strong moisture evident on the walls of most of the rooms.

"I think I need to get up now and eat that one piece of medicine I have in my drawer for fever."

Amar ate that medicine quickly and went off to bed. The moment he laid in the bed, he could hear the loud discussion going on outside.

Look at that moisture on the celling. The first rain has done that. Imagine what would happen if it rained continuously, Mamta said.

It will be worst soon, as it is predicted to have heavy rain from next week onwards. A few days ago, Ram Sagar was asking me about when we were going to paint this house, as his house is having a similar issue with paint coming off the wall. He even recommended me a good contractor who could paint this house for a reasonable price, but he has no idea what we are going through as we barely have enough money to buy small items, Nischint responded.

Yeah, thanks to the gentleman we have in the house for that. If anything happens to this house in this heavy rain, where are we going to live? Will he be able to make enough money in the next six months to get this house painted? said Mamta while raising multiple questions.

All right, I'm going to the office now,said Nischint to Mamta.

"They have started it again. Even the rain is getting me in trouble now. When I was small, I used to enjoy the rain so much that it couldn't be described in words, but today time has turned around so much that the rain is giving me more trouble. I can take medicine to kill this fever, but there is no medicine for what they are saying."

"Well, you have some respite now as Papa is gone to work and Mama is alone." (heavy coughing now)

"Whenever I am coughing, I am having chest pain now. I hope my health will support me for a few more days, as at least once they know the truth, they can support me with my health."

"Imagine if things were normal. By now, Mama would have cooked food and soup for you. Sanskriti would have brought you medicine, and they would be asking you multiple times, How is your health and how are you feeling?"

"Yeah, I am learning a good lesson now about how difficult it is to be alone and manage everything. Whenever I think about it, Uncle Pardeep keeps flashing in my memory."

"It appears that he has become your idol while you are struggling alone."

"Let me eat something before this fever prevents me from even getting up."

He went to eat while unable to stand or walk properly. Mamta saw him struggling with his walk but chose not to say anything. Just a strong stare and a long silence afterwards. Once he gets done with food and back to his bed, he started thinking about something.

"Mama was staring at me as if she wanted to say something but ultimately pulled out of it. I felt like asking her if she wanted to say something, but then maybe my ego pulled me back too."

"Once you told the truth and things got better, maybe one day you could ask her what was going through her mind at that time and if she wanted to say something or not."

"Not only that, but remember when I was going to the doctor for my medical test? A similar situation existed at the time. Maybe one day I'll ask her about all of these incidents. I think that medicine has started kicking in, and I am feeling drowsy now."

"Better cover yourself well, and let's hope you feel better by evening so you can go for your evening walk."

"Yeah, I hope to get out of the house before they start their night discussions and use those strong words against me, which will keep forcing me to overthink lots of things."

"Yeah, that's why you've never felt this tense in your life because whenever they had a complaint about you, they discussed it behind your back, and now that the experiment has made that discussion open, it's bothering you a lot."

"Yes .... Amar dozed off while discussing.

His eyes opened only when they got loud outside.

"It seems like Papa and Sanskriti are back in the house." (coughing heavily with a blocked nose and heavy fever)

"I was expecting to get better with the sleep, but it seems like my fever has gotten heavier now."

"It means you need to listen to their unpleasant music tonight as you can't go out to walk."

"Let them vent out their anger and frustration as only 3 more days are left," Amar said while trying to get up but failing to do so.

"Yeah, luckily, we are in the last leg of the experiment and moving closer to the finish line at a rapid rate."

"Yes, and now let's listen to All Anger Radio," Amar said as he coughed.

How was your work, Nischint? Mamta asked him.

Not that great, to be honest, because I had an argument with Ram Sagar and my mood got off, Nischint replied.

What did he do now? Mamta asked curiously.

It's not totally his mistake, but the way he kept on saying it irritated me a lot. As you know, we are already stressed with what we are facing, and on the top of that, Ram Sagar started asking me why am I not going for house repainting when I told him that our house got moisture due to the rain. Since I can't tell him the truth, I try to avoid answering that, but he keeps persisting with it. Earlier people used to annoy me with what your son is doing, and now they shifted to money matters, replied Nischint which shows his helplessness.

Then how did you end that discussion with Ram Sagar? Mamta asked further.

He kept asking me, which irritated me so much that I told him that I would make my personal decisions when I wanted and he didn't need to be so concerned. I think it hit him, and after that, he didn't talk to me the whole day, and I kept feeling guilty for saying that to him, but I couldn't gather enough courage to say sorry or clarify things , Nischint Answered.

I think you should say sorry to him tomorrow and get on good terms with him. We can't ruin relationships with our friends. I know he (Amar) made us anxious and helpless and we are struggling with even basic needs, but we have to keep friendship with people as who knows when we will be requiring any kind of assistance, including financial one , Suggested Mamta.

Yes, you are right. Tomorrow I will fix that matter, and thanks for a piece of advice that could help me avoid future arguments as well. Anyway, why Sanskriti is still not home ? Nischint inquired.

She is having a small meeting in her school regarding her school trip to a book fair. She must be on her way home, Mamta replied.

"You miss me, and I am here," said Sanskriti as she entered the house.

What made you late today, and how was your trip meeting? asked Nischint.

Well, there were some discussion related to which day trip should be, replied Sanskriti.

So which day are you going? inquired Mamta.

Well, in the end, we have moved the trip a day ahead, and it's going to be on Monday, answered Sanskriti.

Well, that's fine. Take some rest on Sunday and have a good go on Monday, suggested Nischint.

Okay, Sanskriti, come help me with dinner preparation, Mamta invited Sanskriti.

I am going to my room to have some relaxation, Nischint said to Mamta.

"Finally, the discussion is almost over for tonight."

"Yeah, most probably, as they might have a few more things left for dinner."

"Now I can assure them that after three days, they won't get annoyed by anyone with any money-related thing."

"Not only that, but after getting out of this experiment, you could quickly start off teaching students, and then people couldn't annoy Papa by asking what are you doing in life as well ."

"Definitely . I've been in bed for almost 24 hours, fighting a fever, cough, and cold, and no one has even come to my room to look for me."

"Because all of them are worried about their things. Papa is worried about the moisture in the house and avoiding questions related to money. Mama is concerned about any situation in which money is required, as well as about papa's health. Sanskriti is occupied with her trip on Monday and school. Plus they are still full of anger and frustration that money lost has given them. They don't need your presence because your value has dropped to zero and they have nicely distributed your work among themselves as well."

"Yeah, that's why no one asked how am I even though I was in my room whole day and coughing as well ."

"Yeah, (coughing again with chest pain and crying heavily)

After a couple of minutes of heavy crying and a big patch of tears, he has finally controlled it.

"You better stop thinking about it, as the more you cry, the harder it will get for you to get through the remaining 3 days."

"I am facing a lot with my health, and today is the worst day of the experiment as I can't even get up from bed and have my lunch"

"Stop talking about the same thing again and again and crying. You should listen to some music now until they finish dinner, because if you listen to them again, you will cry and your eyes will become extremely swollen."

Amar started listening to music to protect their voice from getting into his ears. Amar is still hearing music even after an hour.

"I think they must be done now, and food must be put there, just as people put food in rat traps."

"The only difference is that once a rat has food, it gets trapped but you have multiple chances."

"The rat dies in one stroke, whereas I die every day."

"I am confident that after these 10 difficult days, we all will see a new Amar who is far stronger, not just physically but mentally, with a proper plan and the ability to execute it as well."

"Most importantly, an independent Amar who is both mentally and financially strong."

"Get ready to get up and eat dinner now as they've gone into their rooms."

After nearly 10 minutes of struggle, he stood up and ready to leave his room .

"Oh, I totally forgot that I didn't even brush my teeth in the morning. not even washed my face."

"First, brush your teeth quickly and wash your face as well ."

Amar brushed his teeth while struggling to even stand up. By the time he finished washing his face, coughing has taken over.

"Too much coughing is going to disturb me the whole night and make me weak."

"Yeah, you better boil some water and have it while eating."(coughing heavily)

He leans against the wall as he is unable to feel confident enough to walk on his feet.

"I won't last long, and I needed to get back to bed."

"First, let's boil water quickly, as coughing is more troublesome than hunger."

Once the water got boiling, he started eating and barely managed to finish it off. He literally dragged himself to the room while carrying that hot water.

"This is the first time in my life I've boiled the water for me despite being so sick."

"Always remember, Amar. Everything happens for the first time, and at this age you should be expecting anything and everything that could happen to you."

After sipping some water, he felt better with his throat and could breathe a bit better.

"Finally, after 24 hours, I get some respite from this gripping cough. I was a dead duck in bed today , I couldn't even go for a walk, and I had to listen to them the entire day."

"Let's hope you get better and go for a walk tomorrow."

"Yes, let's call it a night and stay strong, my heart. There are only three days until this pain goes away."

Finally day 7 of "The Family Experiment" ends and paves way for day 8.

A Surprise unfolds!

Finally, Good Morning from the 9th of April! Why is it a good morning? Because Amar is finally feeling better about his health and his body's energy has returned though he is still in bed and thinking about what to do on the 8th day of the experiment. Suddenly, his phone began to fill up with emails and messages. When he checked them, there was nothing special except for one thing that was common in all of them though there were from various online service providers.

"Wow, I was so busy with my life, especially the last 7 days, that I totally forgot that it is not only the 9th of April but also my birthday."

"Happy Birthday day Amar. How are you going to celebrate it? You are turning 26 today!"

"Thank You but There's nothing to celebrate with the current scenario, but if they wish me happy birthday, I think I'll call the experiment over today."

"Are you sure about it?"

"Yes, I would not remind them, but if they wish, surely that would show their care and love for me, and since they would be nice to me, I would also show my love and care by ending the experiment two days earlier."

"What if they don't wish you intentionally or completely forget about it?"

"Yeah, in that case, one thing is for sure that this experiment is going to last for the full 10 days."

"How about you? You shouldn't waste this special day. You might not have any financial assistance from them like you used to have on your previous birthdays, but certainly you could do something to make it memorable."

"Yeah, I know what to do now. Since my health is better today, I will be happy and forget about all my tensions. I won't cry, feel frustrated, or get angry. I will spend good time in the park, enjoy nature, and even go for jogging in the evening. Try as much as possible to avoid them so that I won't listen to their sharp attack."

"That sounds perfect, and get out of bed now."

"Yeah, let me get done with the shower and finish off my happy breakfast."

As he moved out of his room to have breakfast, he was full of excitement, thinking that they could wish him anytime and it would be like, "Oh, god! It's done and dusted." He got to dinner's table and started waiting for Mamta to see him. He could feel his heart beating fast with excitement.

"She hasn't seen me, and I can't wait for that to happen. That would be the first touch and probably the most important one."

He has eaten half the food, and his nerves are settled.

"I think I am not going to see her now, so I better eat quickly and get out of here."

As he was about to finish it, he got stunned when Mamta noticed him. A few minutes have passed with a long stare, it appears that she has a vague idea of what day it is, but her rage has buried it. The time is up for that fine tension as Amar is back in his room.

"She might not have remembered the date, but surely she was surprised to see me happy because it's the first time I've been happy since this experiment began."

"Yeah, now she would be thinking about it whole day long until she remembers what day it is. Get ready now to enjoy your birthday and put on new clothes as well."

"What should I be doing outside?"

"Well, go with the flow. Just see how things are going on outside and enjoy."

"Alright. Let's have a go."

Amar puts on new clothes and ready to leave happily. As he was leaving, Mamta saw him again with new clothes.

"Usually, I don't put on new clothes and only do it on special occasions. It means new clothes would act as another clue for mama to put stress on her mind to think about what's special today."

When he went outside, the sun was shining brightly with cold breeze. The park was obviously the first place that came to his mind.

As he entered the park, he could hear the loud chirping of birds, as if they were saying, "Happy birthday to you. "

He saw his usual sitting bench and grabbed it.

"Time flies so fast. I still remember how your last year's birthday went."

"Yes, the morning wishes from them, followed by a lovely breakfast consisting of multiple dishes. After that going out for lunch and shopping. Buying cake, balloons, and a variety of other items for the evening. A small but lovely birthday party with a cake cutting ceremony, delicious food, soft drinks, music, dancing, and of course, my favourite moment of receiving and opening gifts."

"Yes, with so many pictures getting clicked and all those lovely memories."

"And look at this year. Nothing at all, not even wishes. Even if they couldn't arrange any of those things where money is involved, they could have wished me, and guess what? I would have ended the experiment after that."

"I think they don't remember it because Papa and Mama could be upset and might not wish you due to anger, but Sanskriti would have wished you regardless of the circumstances."

"Yeah, I also think so. The anger and anxiety about money have taken over their minds so strongly that they don't see anything apart from that."

"If you keep indulging yourself in the past, you will start feeling tense. Today, just enjoy nature and this day. See, even divine powers are with you. Yesterday you were not able to even get up from your bed, and today you are fit and fine. No coughing also"

"Yeah, I noticed that too. Since I will be around this park in the evening as well, I better go somewhere to see something different."

After that, he began walking and looking around. He eventually arrived to a large farm land where he saw people working on the field and some tents erected as well .

"They must be living in those tents, right? Isn't it?"

"Yeah, they must be living in those tents and working here in this farm land, growing vegetables."

"Then we must thank them for the lovely fresh vegetables they are growing and getting to us."

"It would be great if they were paid well for their hard work as well. You could see that they must be from some far away place, employed by the owner of this farm land, and living in those tents, surviving cold, rain, and even summers."

"Yeah, it's a tough life, and..."

As he was going through his thoughts, he saw some kids playing at a corner of the farm land.

"I think these kids live here with their parents."

"Yeah, I believe so. Which game are they playing there?"

"Probably a mix of football, rugby, and handball. Everything is there, and they are totally into it."

"Look at their clothes. It's cold, but they are wearing very thin summer clothes, still chilly weather have no effect on them."

"Yeah, their enthusiasm is taking over this cold weather, and they are smoking away tomorrow's worries. They have nothing to lose, so why worry?"

"Exactly. Enjoy what you have rather than being worried about what you might not have tomorrow."

"Yeah, like I am enjoying today."

Amar sat there and enjoyed their game as if he was watching a professional game. He was certainly impressed by their laughter, shouting, and yelling. There is no proper shelter, no delicious food, and maybe no surety about future ventures, and yet they are playing barefoot in what appears to be a small field with dust flying all around. He kept watching them play for a couple of hours while sitting on a tree branch and enjoying the sunlight. Finally, their game got done when their parents came to them and said something. There is some good distance between Amar and them, so he can't make out what their parents said.

"I think parents would be like, You have played too much. Now have some food as well."

"They might have (loud chuckle by Amar).I don't want to leave here, but it's lunch time, and I'm not going to skip any meals today because it's my birthday."

"Don't be so loud that even those kids are going to hear that it's your birthday."

Amar swiftly moved towards the house and reached in no time.

"This is going to be the third touch between mama and I , and let's see if anything happens."

His heart started beating fast with strong excitement and butterflies in his stomach. He walked in and looked around for her, but he saw nothing.

"I think she is done with lunch and relaxing. Let me have my birthday lunch and feel blessed."

Today, Amar is eating slowly and thoroughly enjoying himself. Maybe he wants Mamta to spot him and give her some clues.

"I am literally giving so many clues today but sadly they are unable to decipher any of them."

"Them? You have given those clues to Mama only."

"Yeah, don't worry, I will drop a few in the evening when Papa and Sanskriti are home."

"Do you really want them to really pick the main thing from those clues?"

"I can't make it so obvious by telling them, but I am trying my best to show that there is something different today."

"Well, have some rest now, as you might be tired."

"Today, no holding back, no tiredness, just positivity, but let's have a birthday rest. Ha, ha, ha... a chuckle."

"Good evening, birthday boy. Get up. The stage is set outside, and we can't wait for more hints."

"Alright, but what hint am I going to give? I have nothing significant to show."

"Since you can't make it obvious and yet you want them to talk about you, you can put on different clothes than those you had in the morning . If Papa and Sanskriti fail to notice, Mama will surely tell them that you had different new clothes on when you went out in the morning."

"Yeah, that's good idea , and I will pass by them showing a big smile."

"You want to make them think about you for the whole evening."

"All I'm doing is giving them the opportunity to wish me today, otherwise, they'll have to wait a whole year."

"Yeah, that sounds perfect. Let's get it done."

Amar did exactly what he planned while passing by all three of them sitting out in the living room.

"I think they might have picked up those clues, and let them enjoy thinking about it. I am all set to enjoy my birthday evening."

"Don't you think something is missing?"

"What is that?"

"You didn't eat anything sweet on your birthday, and I don't think it should be your first birthday without eating anything sweet."

"Well, it won't be, as while returning to the house, I will buy my favourite chocolate, which I always eat on my birthday."

"Yeah, and to give them the strongest and the last clue, you could enter the house while having it in front of them."

"Yeah, that sounds perfect, but as of now, let's enter the park as I am standing and discussing at the entrance of it."

As he entered the park, he noticed that it was not empty today.

"I am early today, and many people are here. Even my favourite bench is occupied."

"You better go for a walk somewhere else, as this place is full and you need some peace."

He kept walking without realising exactly where he was going. It seems like wind is blowing him away. Suddenly he found himself near that farm land again.

"Wow, I think It appears to be my destiny to spend my birthday evening this way."

He looked around and couldn't find anyone on the farm land.

"Where have they gone suddenly? I think it's evening, and surely they can't playing whole day long."

As he was about to move away , he could hear some clappings going on. He looked closely towards one of the tents, where the clappings noise was coming from. He changed his viewing angle and could see some basic decoration, like a mat on the ground and some balloons on nearby trees.

"I think there is some celebration going on. Maybe a birthday party."

"Yeah, listen carefully. You could hear the Happy Birthday sound . Look, they're all out now."

Amar could see all of them dancing out to some music, and some of the kids were tapping plastic buckets as if they were playing some musical instruments.

"It feels surreal, and look, it's gift time for the birthday boy. What's inside?"

"Oh, it seems like some clothes , as the light is not bright there."

"The birthday boy got new clothes. Look at the happiness there, as they are vocal ,loud, hugging each other and parents are looking extremly delighted ."

Amar enjoyed the whole celebration as an uninvited guest.

"Finally, it's time to move to my shelter. Let them enjoy their food in privacy. I don't want them to see me and feel awkward."

"Don't forget to buy the most important clue."

"Yeah, I was totally into their celebration and I forgot about mine."

He rushed to get his favourite chocolate from the nearby shop.

As he approached the shop, he noticed that the owner has closed it and ready to leave. He inquired about his favourite chocolate, to which the shop owner replied, Yes, I have it in stock, but I am getting late to attend a party, so I would be able to give it to you only in the morning.

Today is my birthday, and every year on my birthday, I love to eat it. I would really be grateful to you if you could open the shop again and get me that , Amar requested to the shop owner.

After thinking for a while, the shopkeeper quickly opened the shop and took that chocolate for Amar.

While giving chocolate to Amar, the shopkeeper said, Happy birthday to you Sir, to which Amar replied, "Thank you."

Now Amar is walking towards his house.

"Finally, I got my first birthday wish."

"Yeah, better late than never. At least something is always better than nothing."

After a few minutes of rapid walking, he is near the house.

"Are you sure that they haven't picked up anything out of those clues I have left? They are acting like they have forgotten, but what if they surprise me now? I am feeling anxious now."

"What If you walk in and they say, Surprise! ... Happy…"

"Enough overthinking, let's just say if it happens, it'll be the best surprise of my life, and I'd appreciate them making sure that I get no idea that they remember it."

"You are standing here for almost 5 minutes. Take a deep breath and let's go. You are either surprised or they are surprised when they see you eating chocolate."

Amar waited for a while to feel normal, as his excitement was going over the limit. He finally entered the house.

.........Surprise......

Amar is surprised, as there is no surprise, and he walked in such a sudden way that for a moment they also get shocked. He walked past by them with a smile and took one big bite of chocolate. Both parties got surprised in their own unexpected ways. As Amar reached his room, finally, his anxious excitement took a breather .

"I have given them many clues, but I guess they have totally lost it."

"Anyway, even if they didn't pick the clues, they would surely be puzzled about what happened to you."

"Yeah indeed. It's time to watch a movie to finish off this birthday."

"After the movie, you need to have a birthday dinner as well."

"Yeah, I totally forgot about it. Correct, Correct."

By the time Amar finished his movie, they were done and dusted with dinner and off to their rooms.

"Finally, such a nice peace outside, and now I can be sure that they have forgotten it."

"Well, it's heartbreaking for you, but whatever happens, happens for the good. As soon as you are going to tell them the truth, they will criticise you for that, and then you could also mention that, due to their anger, they didn't wish you as well."

"Yeah, it could be a good deterrent, but do you think it's going to be enough?"

"Perhaps not, but rather than wasting time debating about it, let's have birthday dinner first."

Amar went out to have dinner.

While having dinner, he is constantly thinking about those kids he saw in the farm land today.

"If they can be happy with the least amount of resources while celebrating, why can't I be?"

"You even have a proper shelter on your head" (while looking up at the ceiling.)

Amar enjoyed his dinner at a very slow pace as he was not able to move his mind out of those visuals of the farm land. Finally, he is done with dinner, and before he could move into his room, he took one last look at their rooms.

"Today I have the best birthday ever with the least amount of expenditure. My health got better today. I had three happy meals and learned a good lesson in life: Happiness is not always about spending a lot of money but enjoying what you have."

"Yeah, everything was fine, except that they should have remembered it as well."

"Yeah, but life is also teaching me that time is not going to remain the same forever, and never underestimate the power of money. It can replace anyone in a jiffy."

"Had they remembered it , you would have not gone to that farm land or park and never experienced something like that."

"Yeah, that's why I am saying whatever happens, happens for good."

"All is well that ends well, and today ended very well for you."

"Yeah i did but it would be great if they.........this is first time ....they didn't wish.........on my birthday...."(Ultimately, Amar breaks down a bit with tears in his eyes.)

"Why are you crying when you decided that there would be no crying today?"

"I kept myself high all day and went with the positive flow, but I am not a robot."

"Yeah, but it's almost over, so forget this and think if this money lost can make them forget your birthday, then they're not going to be easy on you after learning the truth."

"Yeah, the signs are quite ominous now, and I need to have a plan about it."

"Tomorrow is the penultimate day of the experiment, and you better have some solution to make them feel that they were wrong too all this while."

"Yeah, tomorrow I will think some idea about it, but now it is time to sleep ."

Finally, a happy and eventful day for Amar after such a long time, and the 8th day is also done. Good night to Amar as we move into the Day 9th of "The Family Experiment."

What a plan!

Good morning from 10th April , where Amar is under pressure to devise some strategies to make them less rigid with him once they learn the truth. He is up and feeling great today.

"There's no sign of cough and cold. It's a miracle that I am feeling so well today."

"Yes, and yesterday's positivity has helped you feel so stress free and relieved."

"Yeah, today I will continue the same positivity, though I need to find a strong solution as well."

"But first things first. Let's get done with the shower and breakfast. Don't forget the big smile, please."

Finally, Amar is done with everything he needs to do before the hard thinking part.

"I think I would better go somewhere else to have a calm, peaceful place to turn on my thinking."

"Where else other than your best friend? Isn't it?"

"Absolutely"

Amar got out of the house and reached the park in no time .

" Yesterday you were busy with other people, and in the evening I was busy watching their birthday celebration that we couldn't meet, but today things are perfect," Amar said to his best friend, which is none other than The Park.

"Let's get ready to start thinking "

Amar grabbed his favourite bench and sat there.

"Right now, I have only one weapon, which is talking about my birthday to them. While telling them the truth, I could use it, but I am not really sure about how effective is it going to be."

"Yes, it can be effective, but if they get really smart, they can neutralise it easily."

"But how is it possible? Isn't it a big thing?"

"Yes, it is a big thing, but right now you are still not sure whether they have forgotten it or intentionally did not wish as a form of showing their anger and how hurt they feel due to their loss."

"Yep, even if they had forgotten it, they can simply label it as an intentional miss. It means that my most powerful weapon can easily be destroyed."

"It can be used, but surely it won't bail you out of that situation for sure."

"Yes, I have to understand that it is going to be an emotional rollercoaster ride for them, so the solution should be such that it should be able to reduce the intensity of that back and forth emotional jerk and work spontaneously"

After understanding the parameters of what kind of solution is needed, he started throwing ideas around and trying to fit them into his requirement mould. He couldn't find a solution that met all of the criterias even after a couple of hours of thinking.

"I think this thing is making me anxious, and I better don't get under pressure."

"Yes, instead of sitting, you better have a walk, as sitting for too long will block your mind."

He started walking here and there but still couldn't think of anything substantial. After a while he realised that its afternoon now and lunch must be ready.

"I think I'll have to sacrifice today's lunch and nap to find the solution, as I don't have much time left."

"Yeah, as tomorrow is the last day, the time is flying , and pressure is slowly creeping up on you."

Finally, he saw something that, which is not a solution, but certainly a sight to behold. He saw those kids of the farm land, going somewhere with their parents.

"Where are they going in the afternoon?"

"I have no idea about it, but have you noticed their happiness?"

"Yeah, happiness and excited faces as if something amazing is about to happen."

"Don't get completely lost in them, and kindly do focus on your things as well."

"Yeah, that's right, but whenever I see them, I completely loose my focus and forget my worries as well."

"Yeah, this experiment has made you more sensitive towards people and their issues, but your own issue is at a critical stage, and you don't have much time left."

"I am tired now, and I better sit on that stone."

"It appears that your mind is either completely frozen or deliberately playing mind games with you."

"Look there, they are coming back."

"Here you go again. You can't focus on your things for a while and tracking them like a radar."

(After few minutes of silence.)

"Why are those three kids crying and stomping on the ground? Take note of the mother's yelling and rebuking."

"All I can think off by looking at them is that they might wanted something, but as their parents said, no, that's why they are crying and stomping on the ground. Look carefully, they are carrying some rice and vegetables as well."

"Yeah, your guess seems absolutely on point. Their small little demands are not met, which is why they are going crazy. Maybe due to financial condition."

As they get closer, he can see the mother's anger getting higher, with some support from the father as well. Kids are getting louder with their crying and hitting the ground more and more.

"I can't stand here like this because it might make them uncomfortable. I should do something instead of standing here like a statue, so they don't get the impression that I'm just here to watch them."

He quickly took out his phone and pretended to be on a phone call so that he could clearly hear what was going on when they pass by. As they passed by Amar, with kids yelling, crying, and refusing to go home at any cost, both father and mother were yelling and pushing them forward to make them walk.

"Luckily, the father or mother didn't beat any of them, though they were annoying as hell and very close to getting beaten. Even though they were so close to me, I couldn't figure out exactly what made them cry."

"Whatever the reason, both parties are going against each other. Kids are adamant with their demands and have no intention of going home without their demands being met, and parents could have their problems and find themselves unable to fulfil their demands while trying their best to take them home."

"What do you think is going to happen? How long will they be crying? Parents were also enraged, so they may run out of patience and beat them as well."

"Right now, my mind is totally messed up, and I can't come up with any possible prediction for them."

"I can't think about anything other than them now, as my curiosity is going beyond everything as well. I'm also concerned that if those kids are beaten up by their parents, they won't be as vivid and happy as they were yesterday."

"I think you're overthinking a lot, and due to this, you are not able to find any solution for your own problem .It's good that you are becoming concern for society, but charity begins at home."

"Yes, and I won't be going home without getting some solution for my problem as well, but right now my mind is not able to think anything apart from what is going to happen with those kids."

"I believe your mind will not be at ease until you learn what they are facing, so it's fine if you take some time, walk to that farm land, and learn what exactly happened rather than speculating and wasting your time."

Amar went to the farm land after obtaining his own permission to do so. Enthusiasm and Excitement were at such a high peak that he reached there quickly. Once he reached there, he saw, at one corner, those three crying kids sitting, stomping and digging the ground in anger. Parents are near those tent houses, cooking some food, and yelling at them loudly.

"I still believe that no party is ready to give up, and things are still quite heated."

"I think if parents try to coax them rather than being coercive in nature, those kids would stop their stubborn protest."

"Yes, that is true, but if they get mild immediately, the kids will use this crying as a tool against the parents, which is why they have to be harsh as well."

Amar kept staring at them from a tree branch, which provided him with a good vantage point. After a while, he noticed that food was ready, and parents took food out on plates. Those plates are made out of tree leaves. The next moment, he could see both father and mother carrying something in a bucket.

"What are they doing now? Kids are still crying, but parents have calmed down now. What are they carrying in bucket?"

"Well, keep an eye and let's see how they handle them."

The next moment, he could see parents trying to wash their kid's feet, as they were totally into dirt. Kids are still not ready to give up, but somehow they manage to wash their feet and put on slippers.

"They are really smart as they started with washing their feet to make them feel better rather than offering them food, which they would have denied for sure."

"They might not be aware of this, but this is clearly a marketing trick where you hook customer at cheaper price of a product and then increase it slowly by adding a few more terms and conditions."

Now they slowly take them to tents where food is being kept.

"See now, they are coaxing them with maximum efforts to make them eat their first bite. As they start eating, they would totally forget about what was going on 10 minutes ago."

As Amar could see, both Mother and Father were trying to feed them with their hands, caress their heads, and hug them to make them feel better. After a few NOs, they finally gave up, everyone is eating food, and calmness has taken over.

"It's hard to believe that these are the same parents who were so hard on them that they were on the verge of bearfnmting them, but look how sweet and nice they are to their children now. And look at those kids. You can't even hear a single noise now. Now my mind can stay at peace as this is what we could call a happy ending."

"Their happy ending is complete, and if you want something similar on Monday, you better come up with something because the sun has begun to set and evening has arrived."

Amar has started his walk towards the house. While on the way, he is thinking about how time and people can change.

"One thing that is common between my parents and their parents is money. I lost money that's why they are harsh at me, and those parents were harsh at kids because they might not have enough money to fulfil their demands."

"And as soon as they realise that kids aren't old enough to understand finance, they coax them with love and care."

"Earlier my parents were so harsh at me also, but then for the past two days, the intensity has gone down as I am not going in front of them a lot."

"They may not be showing it, but the rage must be boiling like lava does in a volcano calmly, and what happens when a volcano erupts?"

"All that heated lava comes out, and it calms down completely for many years."

"Exactly. They may be angry, but not angry enough to vent all their rage in the form of lava."

"You mean I make them even more angry and let them vent their rage so that when I tell them the truth on Monday, they'll have nothing to say?"

"I am not saying that you make them tired by making them angry, but all you have to do is exactly the opposite of what you have been doing for the past few days."

"Okay, I have understood the whole plan now. Instead of leaving or hiding inside the room, I will simply remain in their vision for the entire day tomorrow, which will undoubtedly increase their rage to a new level."

"The best part is that tomorrow is Sunday, which means Papa and Sanskriti both will be home. So, tomorrow, they would vent out their anger at you and get extremely harsh with you. When you tell them the truth the next day, they will realise that they were so harsh on you the day before and will immediately feel guilty. To cover their harshness, they would coax you, just like those kids parents did , and after two or three days, they would totally forget about this Experiment or the things associated with it."

"Yes, and I could also use my other weapon of birthday omission as well to support my statement with the big surprise that money is totally safe with me."

"What an excellent idea it is, but everything comes at a cost. The cost associated with it is that you have to go through such a harsh condition with very sharp words hitting your heart again and again."

"Well, I am well trained now for that, and it is just the last time I have to face it. Tomorrow, as I have decided that there is no escape for me to move out of the house, I won't be able to see my best friend, The Park as well ."

"Yes, it means the next time you meet your best friend, this experiment would be over. So before you go home, it would be great to say thank you to your best friend, The Park, for always allowing you to have peace of mind there."

Amar went to the park and grabbed his favourite bench. He looked around to see trees, plants, and tiny flowers.

"Dear Park, thank you for being nice to me. You gave me nice hospitality and accommodations when my life was having a big storm. When I couldn't find peace or take their verbal strike, I came here and felt safe. Thank you so much for everything. I know it's time for me to go, but I promised to come back here on Monday to see you again."

As Amar started walking away, he turned around one last time to see his favourite bench and things around it, as he believes that these things belong to him. He stared at them for over five minutes as if he wouldn't get the chance to see them again, and now he started walking away with teary eyes.

"Finally, my day is coming to an end, and tomorrow will be the last day of The Family Experiment, and everything is planned and set."

"Yes. When you got out of the bed in the morning, there was such a huge pressure on you, but as the day went on, you found a good solution for such a peculiar situation. Let's hope that things don't go awry, as you won't have time to fix them."

"They would be surprised to see me getting home early, though I have been out whole day."

As Amar entered the house , they were sitting in the living room. They are loud enough that Amar could hear them despite being in his room and not paying attention to that .

"You have two choices right now: listen to them now or listen to them tomorrow at full blast."

"I'm going to discount myself today and mentally prepare for tomorrow's full blast."

Amar puts earpieces in his ears with music on to avoid their voices.

"Tomorrow is the day I have been waiting for so long. I still remember how I felt when it was day number 1. Just a few days into the experiment, I was ready to give up and started begging them to give me a chance to rectify my mistake so I could end this experiment, but nothing happened."

"Yeah, and ultimately things improved when you put some effort into going out and avoiding them."

"Yeah, I had the best birthday ever and got to meet new friends at the farm land and enjoyed their lovely party as well"

"That's all in the past, so what are your plans for tomorrow?"

"I think I will go with the flow, as I don't need to do any planning for tomorrow. I just need to be more visible to them, and the rest will be done by them ."

"Yeah, it sounds perfect. Now all you need to do is have dinner and just go through this sleep to experience the last day of this experiment."

"Yes, I can't believe I have made through it. Tomorrow, once I am in this bed in the evening, I will be thinking about Monday. After telling them the truth on monday , I want to breathe in the fresh air of liberty and get out of this incarceration."

After this, Amar finished his dinner quickly and was ready to go to sleep.

"I think I should be sleeping now, but I completely forgot about the money I kept under my pillow. Let's take a look at them because they would be going into the bank on Monday, and tomorrow I might be so tired of those diatribes that I might forget to check them."

Amar took a quick look at the cash and found it to be exactly as he had left it.

"Everything is fine, and finally I am ready to go to sleep and teleport to the last day of the experiment."

"Are you forgetting anything before you start dreaming?"

"As far as my memory goes, there is nothing left apart from setting an early alarm as I needed to be ready early to make sure things are going well."

Amar sets an early alarm, the earliest alarm since this experiment started, and off he goes to sleep.Now we are all ready to move on to 11th April , the last day of this experiment.

Good morning from the final day of "The Family Experiment." It's Sunday, and probably this is the earliest he has ever gotten up due to the excitement.

"First, let me sink in the fact that today is the last day of the experiment. All those hard yards I covered have come to an end."

"There is no need to think about how things went and please get done with your shower as today you needed to be in the spotlight in front of them, which means you have to join them for breakfast as if they have invited you."

Amar finished off the shower and other activities in a jiffy and all set for breakfast.

"I am in such a rush that they are still sleeping and i cant wait to join them for breakfast."

"Yes, now relax, calm your mind down, and be ready for an impact as strong as the initial impact you had when you told them about the loss."

"Yeah, and to play smart, I could divide the whole day into three sessions. Session one is going to have the morning, Session two will have the afternoon, and Session three is the longest one , with the evening and night. Each passing session will give me more and more hope that I'm nearing the end."

"Yes, now keep listening to what is going outside, as I can hear they are up now."

"Yes, let me have good concentration on what is being discussed outside so I can go out exactly when they have breakfast and surprise them."

Amar waited for quite a while, as things were quite slow outside due to the day being Sunday. Finally, that time has come after an eternity .

"It's time to start off session number 1. Let's take a deep breath, and here comes the plunge."

As Amar came out, they were not expecting him to join them. They were in total shock as he pulled out one chair and sat there.

"How is your school going on Sanskriti?" asked Amar.

As he joined , they were in shock, but the moment he asked this question, they started looking at each other's faces in total disbelief. Amar pulled out a plate, took some vegetables and roties(wheat tortilla), and started eating. After a few minutes of silence, it was finally broken.

You don't need to be so worried about her school or about our worries. You are getting food. Just have it and move away from here, Mamta said angrily.

I'm just asking her a simple question, that's all , Amar responded to Mamta.

As Mamta calmed down, Amar again asked Nischint, How is your health going on?

You don't need to be worried about anything related to us. It would be a great help if you don't talk to us, make us annoyed, and stay away from our matters, then our health would be okay, said Nishcint while folding his hand in front of Amar.

He is talking as if he has earned a fortune for us, which we could use to fix our health or get this leaking house fixed. Forget about earning a single rupee, he has lost what we have saved. Now we have nowhere to go, Mamta added to Nischint's retort.

There is no need to argue with him as he is using all his energy to destroy us completely. He has destroyed us financially, and now he is taking our health away as well, said Nischint while looking at Mamta.

This strong criticism has hit Amar very hard, and he couldn't stay there even for a moment. He quickly finished breakfast and off to his room.

While going into his room, he could hear Sanskriti saying, "Mummy and Papa, why are you responding to him? He is just draining your energy to satisfy his frustration of not being able to do anything in life."

Now Amar is in his room; the coughing is back, and he is about to break down as well.

"Amar, I know it's hard for you, but you can't break down now as it's not even one session. Just stay strong and hold these tears."

"See, just a few minutes into that negativity, coughing and chest pain have returned."

"It's just the last day, and you have to follow what you have planned. Just hang on."

Amar took a sigh of relief, washed his face, and whipped it off as well.

"Should I wait here now or go out again?"

"I think you should wait for a while now, and then you can go there as they are sitting, and instead of talking to them, you can watch TV there."

"I didn't watch........... (coughing heavily Now).

After a few minutes, when he felt a bit better, he went out and turned on the TV and started watching it. As TV noise started interfering with what they were discussing, they decided to go into the rooms as they were not expecting Amar to start watching TV in front of them.

"I think they are using my trick on me by simply avoiding me."

"Yes, it seems like they have learned this trick from you."

We are not getting any peace on Sunday either, in our own house. Fortunately, we don't live in a house he built, Amar overheard Mamta said to Nischint.

"Don't worry, soon there will be only peace in the house," said Amar to himself.

Amar spent about an hour watching TV, and when he got sure that they were not coming out of their room, he turned off the TV and went to his room.

"I think session one is done, as I don't think they are going to face you again before lunch."

"Yes, it was hard initially, but I think... (coughing)... it's hard, but as it's the last day, let it be the hardest."

"Yeah, you better take some rest before you face some heat again."

"Yeah, that's right, as I can feel pain on the left side of my chest and my lips are getting dry as well."

"Better rest now, otherwise, even on the last day, criticism could severely impact your health."

Amar slept in bed and closed his eyes, as he was feeling low energy. He was feeling so lethargic and fell asleep. Finally,their outside noises disturbed his sleep, luckily he got up and looked at the wall clock in his room.

"Thank God that I didn't sleep the whole afternoon, otherwise, the plan would have gone awry."

"It seems like they are getting ready for lunch, and session two starts now."

"It could be intense, but I think it won't last long because most probably they will disappear again after lunch."

"Let's see how it goes."

Amar went out, and this time they are not surprised because they knew that he is not going to leave them alone today. While eating with them, Amar suddenly asked, "How long will you not be talking to me as we all live in the same house?" They ignored him totally, as if there was no one there except three of them. Amar was irritated because there was no response from their end. He kept eating food and was about to finish it off.

"The lunch was very delicious, but unfortunately I had to eat it alone." Amar took a dig at them, but they were also very adamant not to say even a single word. Amar is done with lunch, but they are still eating at such a pace that half of the their food is still on the plate.

"I think I should wait here while they are eating. There could be a chance that they would finally open their mouth", Amar thought in mind.

This is probably the first time in these 10 days that they have totally stayed silent. They quietly kept eating, and the moment they got done, they left Amar over there and decided to shut the doors.

"Wow, what a strategy they have deployed to counter my plan. It appears that they were aware of my plan and have devised a counter-plan."

"I think there is no plan here from them. It is quite possible that they might be running out of words. For the past 10 days, they have used every single issue they could have raised to vent out their anger."

Since it is going to be complete peace out there so Amar is back in his room now.

"Since today is the last day of the experiment , I will be bringing this new change into my life by avoiding the afternoon nap ."

"Yeah, and it would also help you get good sleep at night due to the fact that you would get a bit more tired."

"Let's lie down in bed and wait until I can hear them outside."

Amar has set the alarm just in case he falls asleep accidentally.

"Tomorrow, by now, I would be in a totally different situation. Since I've decided not to nap, I could use that time to visit my best friend The Park, jog there, enjoy nature, and calmness."

"How about the chest pain you keep having from time to time?"

"Well, I think I have taken too much verbal beating on my heart, and I feel that due to this, it has become quite weak and easily starts pumping fast as soon as I hear their criticism."

"Maybe not tomorrow, but when things get settled down between you and them, then you could visit a cardiologist."

"Yeah, hopefully the cardiologist's piece of advice, coupled with regular visits to the park and less stress on me, could fix that pain as well."

"Just one more session to go, and surely the longest one of today as well."

"The first session was way tougher for me as I was under the pump, but the second one was totally quiet. I'm not going to make any predictions about the third one, but no matter how difficult or quiet it gets, the excitement of finishing this experiment is the highest."

"Yes, and once you're in bed again tonight, you can draw conclusions about what you've learned and how it will help you shape your future."

"Not only that, but I could avoid a lot of future mistakes as well from what I have learned in the last 10 days. I have a strong feeling that these 10 days of suffering have transformed me from a boy to a man, who will be able to handle pressure in a much better way and can perform strongly as well by getting out of his comfort zone."

After a couple of hours,

"I think they are up, and you better get ready also. The first two sessions were pretty bleak, so make sure this one is a bit more active."

Amar quickly got out before they could take their positions and sat there. Finally, the stage is set, with three of them on one side and Amar on the other. Now Amar is there with no intentions of escaping, and they can't escape anywhere. Both parties are tensed as they stare at each other, wondering who will say the first few words. Amar can't hold himself back for long, as staying quiet is like following their plan.

"Don't worry. We will be getting back the amount I have lost in a few months time. Maybe I will make a little more than what I have lost," said Amar to target them.

Finally, this thing has rekindled the fire that has gone dormant since the morning. The floodgates are open now .

"Forget about making that whole amount, I can guarantee that he couldn't even make 1% in the next six months. Your mind functions best when you are destroying things. Destroy this and that. That's it," Nischint responded while looking at Mamta.

"Someone who is sitting in front of us with pride and annoying us by being here without any shame is surely born to be maleficent for us." Mamta fueled the fire even more.

"I can assure you, Mamta, that he is not going to do anything in life, and I can give it in writing as well. You can laminate that writing and stick it on this wall," Nichint said loudly, coughing now.

As soon as Sanskriti saw it, she was quick enough to give Papa some water and calm him down.

Please move out of here now as Papa is getting furious and losing his mental peace, requested Sanskriti to Amar.

I am tired of these daily criticisms and not able to concentrate on anything in life, said Amar in an angry tone.

And we are tired of your daily lies. Had we not placed this much trust on you, we would not have lost our fortune, Mamta responded angrily.

Don't test our limits, otherwise, either you would be living here alone or we would be living here alone, said Nischint with a distorted voice.

Things have gotten quite intense. Amar is maintaining a hard and resolute personality, though he is crying deeply from the inside. He could feel his heart getting swollen due to receiving constant hits, but he is staying in the battle field as it is the last session of the last day of the experiment. His inner voice keeps telling him to keep going, and can take this criticism easily.

Now that we only have one child, I am confident in her ability to handle all houseworks and take care of us through life's ups and downs. Isn't it Sanskriti? Mamta took a jab at Amar while looking at Sanskriti.

Sanskriti did not respond to this question.

It would be great if we had only one child since the beginning of time, as the other one has destroyed us from top to bottom. Someone's existence has jeopardised our future existence, Nischint raged.

Yes, you are absolutely spot on. We always managed things so well with limited resources, but today we have become beggars. If something happens, we have to kneel in front of people and ask for help, Mamta said, putting the final nail in the coffin.

Amar realised that his chest pain was creeping up at a rapid rate and he could collapse anytime if he stayed there for even 10 seconds. He rushed into his room without a word and laid in his bed while holding his chest.

"I think I'm done with them for tonight. I can't take it anymore, both physically and mentally."(Coughing slightly)

"Yeah, you can relax now that the experiment is over. Congratulations on surviving!"

Right now, Amar is catching his breath, feeling chest pain, and battling with occasional coughing. You can imagine his condition as if he has fought ten rounds of a boxing match without rest. They are still having strong word play outside, but Amar is not paying any attention to it.

"Now I am going to stay in and go out only when they are done and dusted with dinner so I can have my eating part as well."

Amar spent a couple of hours lying in bed to feel better, but it seems like his health has refused to give him any respite on the last day of the experiment.

"I don't think this pain will go away, and since they appear to be in their caves, let's have an early dinner because I can't wait until tomorrow morning."

"Before you can enter a new morning, there must be some analysis and conclusion about this experiment."

"Yes absolutely"

In the next ten minutes, we saw Amar's struggle to get out of bed while holding his chest, walk all the way to the dinner table, and eat with one hand while keeping the other on his chest.

"The pain is getting severe now, but nothing could be bigger than successfully going through these 10 days. I wish I would never enjoy any food like this in my life."

Amar tried his hardest to eat as much as he could, but the severe chest pain didn't help him much.

Finally, he is done with dinner, a mere formality as he didn't have much. Now that he's in bed and wants to take a look at the treasure he's kept hidden under his pillow before he starts thinking about anything.

"Hash, they are safe and sound. It is now time to keep them out of the pillow."

Amar put them on one side of the bed because there is no fear of someone seeing them now as the experiment is over.

"This small bag of money has given me all the physical and mental pain, reducing my value in this family to zero, and I am literally dead for this family. Tomorrow, as soon as this bag gets into their hands, I will be alive for them, my value will rise, and all this stress and pain I have in life is going to perish."

"Well, enough criticism of this bag of money , and you better have some analysis about the outcome of this experiment because the pain is increasing and you won't be able to last long enough."

"No pain can kill the excitement of getting it done and learning so many lessons in just 10 days. The message is loud and clear: Money is a very important part of life. It can't be ignored at all. Human values, family values, love and care revolve around it. If you are constantly making it, your value in the family will remain relevant, whereas losing it will reduce your value to zero."

"Yes, and furthermore, it has the power to make big chances in a jiffy. It took just a few hours to drop your value and respect in this family to zero after you told them about the loss. The value, respect, and trust you built over many years were turned into rubble."

"Ahhh...... This pain is too much for me to bear. Tomorrow, if it stays like this, I need to see a cardiologist. Forget about outside people, despite understanding me so well, they never got ready to give me a second chance in life, though I am young and surely could have recovered it even if I lost in real ."

"Consider yourself lucky that it was just an experimental lie. Had it happened in the real world, by now you would most probably be dead."

"Yes,,,,,,',holding chest tightly with tears coming out now.

Amar wiped those tears .

"Yeah, and now I have understood that if I have to maintain my value in this family for the long term, then I have to start making money and try to make it quickly as well. The faster I make money, the more valuable I will become to my family and for the world as well. I've reached that point in my life and age where doing housework and assisting others will not help me gain respect in my family. The respect is directly proportional to the amount I....."(coughing heavily)

"If you can't take it, tell them now that your health is going down."

"If I could survive that long, then I can survive one more night as well. Now that this experiment is over, my entire focus will be on making money, and the best part is that I know exactly how to do it."

"Well, that's good. How about if they are still angry even after knowing the truth?"

At the moment, Amar could feel his lips getting dry. He drank a good amount of water.

"When I can take their full blast of anger for 10 days, then surely their anger after knowing the truth would have no impact on me, and on top of that, all these problems happened due to money, so as soon as I make money through teaching, they will forget everything. If this money can turn me into a zero, it will turn me into a hero once I start making it."

"Tomorrow would be so different from the previous 10 days, and finally, freedom."

"Yes, and I would meet my best friend The Park and spend some time there as well "(Amar exclaimed, raising both of his hands in excitement before quickly lowering them due to pain)

Amar went to the mirror to take a look at himself.

"Just look at you, Amar, It seems like you have aged 10 years in the span of 10 days. Those swollen eyes, falling hairs, pulled-in cheeks, lost weight, and dried lips are telling the saga of what you have gone through these 10 days."

"Yes, but not anymore because I made a vow tonight that this boy Amar will vanish tonight and a new Amar will appear tomorrow who will be strong mentally and financially independent as well ."

"Well, it's all good now. Your suffering has made you understand the value of money in life and initiated a new life journey for you. Since it's all ended, it's time for you to take a good, deep sleep with a stress-free mind, and tomorrow just hand over the money to them and tell the truth as well."

"Yeah, and hopefully it goes smoothly, as I can't take their criticism anymore ... (pain in the chest and coughing again). I don't think I need an alarm to get up early because this excitement will not let me sleep until very late in the morning."

"Any last few words before you finally go into deep sleep?"

"Congratulations, My Dear Friend Money, on winning and proving me wrong all together; it only took you a few days to make me dead for my family. Now, I will always respect you." (coughing with pain creeping up)

After a pause.

"I am sorry, Mom, Dad, and Sanskriti, for annoying you, but I had no other option. At the same time, I want to thank those farm land people, the park, the bench i sit on and even my inner voice, which helped me throughout the experiment.

"Okay, Amar, no more talking now, and enjoy the liberty now."

Amar closes his eyes, as the last day of the experiment is also done.

Nigh is near, A happy one?

Shhhhhhhh……….. Quiet please.

It's a new morning, and Amar is sleeping peacefully. His sleep is so deep that he is not bothered by their loud noises today. Finally, a loud bell sound got their attention. It's the doorbell.

Yamraaj is here!

Papa, Yamraaj uncle, is here, said Sanskriti.

What are you preparing for? Yamraaj asked Sanskriti a question.

Uncle, we are going on a school trip and I am getting ready for that, Sanskriti responded.

How are you, Yamraaj, and how come are you suddenly here in the morning? Nischint, surprised, asked.

Yes, everything is alright, and you have no idea how I passed the last night to get here in the morning, Yamraaj responded.

What happened suddenly that was making you so excited the whole night, and you couldn't wait for the night to get over? asked Nischint with a chuckle.

Well, I have two pieces of good news: one for me and the other for you. Which one do you want to hear first? Yamraaj asked.

Ha ha ha, you're having two happy news, which is why you're carrying such a large box of ladoo (Indian dessert), Nischint took a cheeky dig.

I can assure you that once you know the news, you will be jumping as well. But first, tell me where is Amar? Excited Yamraaj inquired.

The moment Nischint heard about Amar ,his excitement jumped off from an aeroplane without parachute. After a couple of seconds of silence, Nischint realised that Yamraaj has no idea what is going on in his house.

Yeah, he is in his room and sleeping. I can't wait to know the good news. Tell me what's good news for you, Nischint said while deftly avoiding any more questions about Amar.

You won't believe it, and no one could believe it, but Akshat scored the highest marks in his class in the high school exam,Yamraaj was over the moon while saying it.

Wow! Congratulations to both you and Akshat. When he met with an accident, I was worried about him that how he would pass the exam, but he did it, said Nischint while hugging Yamraaj.

Yes, I had the same worries, but what a tremendous teaching job by Amar! Akshat could have flunked the exam but ended up topping the whole class. The result was released yesterday evening, and I have received numerous calls from the parents of Akshat's friend asking me who taught Akshat while he was injured because this time the exam was much tougher than the usual standard, and despite that, he performed way better than what everyone expected, including his school teachers, Yamraaj said while handing Nischint a ladoo.

What is the second good news that you said is for me? asked Nischint with a mouthful of ladoo.

The second good news is that Amar has secured his future as well, said Yamraaj with a sense of joy.

What do you mean by securing the future? Nischint is perplexed.

Remember what I just mentioned? I received a tonne of calls in the evening from parents asking me about who taught Akshat. Then I told them it was Amar who taught Akshat for two months while he was injured and couldn't go to school. It was his passionate teaching that helped Akshat achieve academic success. Then they all requested that I ask Amar to give tuition classes to their children as well for this academic year. Trust me, I have secured 50+ students for Amar, with each paying him 3000 rupees a month, explained Yamraaj.

Nischint can’t believe what he is hearing. Maybe for the first time in the past 10 days, he could feel that Amar was not bluffing when he said he could recover the loss. As Nischint was about to get lost in his thoughts, Yamraaj tapped on his shoulder.

What are you thinking? Even if Amar teaches only 50 students at 3K per head, that's 150K a month. He would be making more than we do, said Yamraaj with a giggle.

I know what you are thinking. You are thinking, How could Amar start making such a big amount in a jiffy? Well, you all have always underestimated his knowledge. All this while he might have never made money, but he kept accumulating knowledge, and now he gets what he deserved, Yamraaj said this while noticing that Nischint was not paying full attention to what he was saying.

I know it's a dreamlike thing for you, my brother, but it's true. Anyways, keep this ladoo (Indian dessert) box and share this good news with Sanskriti and Mamta as well. Give this news as a surprise to Amar and ask him to call me in the evening so that he can tell me on which date he would like to start teaching them. I am getting late for work now and will see you some other time, said Yamraaj while walking towards the door.

Once he reached the door, he said, "Congrats Nischint, In less than one year's time, Amar would become a millionaire, and don't forget my party, as you didn't even invite me to Amar's birthday party."

After giving this shocking good news ,Yamraaj is off to his work.

Nischint is completely frozen now. It seems as if his soul has left his body and only muscles and bones are left. One side of his mind is calculating Amar's big money success, and the other half is telling him that he failed to see his real value despite Amar's constant efforts and begging to give him a chance to recoup all the losses, and they became so blind with the money loss that they totally forgot about his birthday as well. It is happening exactly as Amar has planned, the only difference being is that Amar hasn't told them the truth. The money that made him the villain of the family is going to make him a hero now. The eagerness to correct his mistake is clearly visible on Nischint's face . Before he could think about anything else, Sanskriti was out of her room and ready to leave.

What happened, papa? What did Yamraaj Uncle say? Sanskriti inquired.

Yamraaj was here , early morning. Is everything alright? Mamta added further as she was done with her shower as well.

He was here because Akshat topped the high school exam in his class, and they are giving full credit to Amar's two months of teaching. Parents of other students also want Amar to teach their children for the entire academic year because of Akshat's incredible academic success. He also told me that more than 50 students are interested in being taught by Amar for 3000 rupees per head, Nischint informed both of them.

150,000 a month, is that what Uncle Yamraaj meant, Papa? Sanskriti, surprised, asked.

Yeah, that's what he meant, and he also gave us this box of ladoos(Indian Dessert), Nischint clarified.

Now all three are stunned, and there is a deafening silence

Nobody wants to say anything, and suddenly Sanskriti broke that silence with her question, Now what are you thinking to do, Mummy and Papa?

I think we have made a big mistake by not understanding him. He has been begging and requesting that we trust him, and gave him a chance to rectify his mistake, but we never listened to him. We didn't wish him on his birthday and labelled him as robber and criminal. We became completely blind due to the financial loss that we suffered. We forgot that human value is always higher than money value because money can be made again, but our unmerciful behaviour can never be reversed. It would take him less than four months of teaching to make up for what he has lost, but it could take us our entire lives to restore things to their former state. The one we thought as coal turned out to be a diamond, under immense pressure.We failed to understand our own son. I am ....(Nischint coughing..)

Mamta has completely lost her senses and not able to find words to speak anything.

The clouds of silence have taken over again and Nischint is unable to think what to do next to fix their mistake.

I know we have made a big mistake that couldn't be rectified, but there is nothing wrong with apologising to Bhaiya (brother). When Bhaiya (brother) lost money, he at least tried to apologise to us, even though we were as firm as rocks and never listened to him. So this time we were too harsh on him, so we could try to apologise to him. Whether he forgives us or not is in his hands, but we should at least try once with full force, suggested Sanskritii.

They both listened to her carefully but were still in total shock and showed no reaction. It seems like their mind is listening but not responding. It's the same kind of feeling where the mind is ready to accept the truth but the heart is saying, How could you do that?

Papa, you need to go to work, and I have to leave the house in a few minutes for my school trip, said Sanskriti.

I know it's hard for you to accept it, but somehow you both need to get up and let's go to Bhaiya's (brother) room, Sankriti added further.

We have witnessed many times how Amar struggled to get up from bed to get to the dinner table, and now it is exactly the same for Nischint and Mamta. Finally, they are up on their feet, and Sanskriti is guiding them as they are temporarily blind. Their legs are feeling so heavy that even a snail could outrun them easily. Finally, they have reached the door of Amar's room. Now they could feel exactly how Amar used to feel whenever he used to enter the house while they were sitting outside. Their hearts are pumping at a much faster rate, and time has literally stopped for them.

Papa and Mama, we are about to enter Bhaiya's(brother) room. Just don't think a lot, and you both can stay in his room longer as I need to leave for my school trip now, Sanskriti briefed them.

As she opened the door, it was very quiet and calm. As they look at Amar, he is in deep sleep with a big smile on his face. He has the same smile he was born with. The happiness of going through the experiment successfully is written all over his face. No sign of stress or anxiety. Just a pure, innocent smile.

What's that? said Sanskriti while pointing out to the poly bag.

When Nischint took a closer look, he lost the ground beneath his feet.

There is so much money in his room, and what is it? A letter? said Nischint when he finally saw it.

What letter is that? Nischint was inquired by Mamta.

Nischint put on his reading glasses and started reading.

"Dear Mom and Dad, I know you are extremely hurt by the news that I ended up losing 500k rupees in the form of investment. I am touched by your behaviour and the support you have provided me in this hard time. Even though I have lost money, you are still rooting for me and believing that I will be able to recoup it. I even appreciate Sanskriti's support despite knowing that this loss has put her art college plan at jeopardy.

(Sanskriti is trying to wake Amar up. Bhaiya (brother), get up. It's late in the morning.)

Firstly, I would like to sincerely apologise for lying to you all and telling that I lost the money in crypto investment, but the truth is that they are safe with me, and I have hidden them into my pillow in my room.

Now you all would be thinking, Why did I lie about money and waited this long to tell you the truth?

The answer lies in the environment I was facing. I could see things happening around me that made me question my beliefs about human values, respect, and money. As I am growing, I can feel that respect and human values are getting weaker. Money and earning more and more money tend to pull respect and human values up. I was clearly thinking about what your reaction would be if you find out that I have lost the large saving we had set aside for Sanskriti's higher education.

I thought a lot about it before proceeding, as I could see even before this , throughout my life, you have all been very supportive to me and have always stood by my side. I still chose to proceed with it as my mind couldn't settle or be ready to believe what I witnessed happening in the outside world versus the world I have formed through you all. I want to settle it for once and all.

Though it has troubled you all a lot, it has fully restored my faith in family and human values, and your behaviour has proven that money is important but it can never set the love and respect we have in our family apart.

(At this point, Sanskriti has realised that Amar is not responding. She is yelling loudly that Papa and Mummy, Bhaiya(Brother) is not responding, but Nischint is completely lost in reading the letter, and Mamta is speechless with what she is hearing. The whole letter is getting drenched in Nischint Tears. Seeing them giving no response to her yelling, Sanskriti rushed outside to call an ambulance.)

Since I could see happiness on your faces since I started teaching, I would further give my best to find students and try to pursue a career in the teaching world. I promise you that I will never lie again and disturb you like this. I am truly satisfied with the love and care I have in the family."

Your obedient Son,

Amar.

The letter is finished, but the flood of Nischint's tears are still going strong. He is standing there like a dead body, whereas Mamta has lost her sanity.

10 minutes later, The ambulance siren broke the silence. They are still statues in Amar's room, unable to think anything clearly or make any movement . Amar is being taken into the ambulance with his smile still on. Now the ambulance is running away from the house and passing by his best friend the Park and farm land in vain!

About the Author

Mayank Chamoli

Mayank Chamoli was born in 1996 in the city of Dehradun , in a lower middle class family. Through his journey from Lower Middle Class to Middle class, helped him not only to witness the Economic Change but how life changes with it as well. Studied Hospitality in Singapore and been to Malaysia, Indonesia and Sri Lanka gave him a good view of different societies. Being the hospitality student and worked as an intern in the reputed The Ritz Carlton Hotel, Singapore helped him a lot to see how money and social status work.

Though interested in writing fiction, only characters are fictional in nature but their characteristics are either experienced or closely observed by Mayank Chamoli. Facing many failures at different stages of life helped him to understand the pain ,sorrow and implications associated with it and how difficult it gets to work hard without getting taste of success which is reflected in his writing as well.

Printed in the USA
CPSIA information can be obtained
at www.ICGtesting.com
LVHW082313041123
762866LV00006B/218

9 789357 878647